BARABANKI

A frequent TEDx speaker and and an entrepreneur, Anuj Tiwari was brought up on the bustling streets of Bareilly and Lucknow. Tiwari studied in a Hindi-Sanskrit-medium school where there were no English books. Seeing the kids of his neighbourhood read colourful storybooks, he started building dreams of being able to read in English; however, he kept those dreams to himself.

Despite going through six months of depression and severe anxiety, and trying to give up on his life in college, Tiwari is now the bestselling author of several books, inspired by real-life incidents. In 2014, he was adjudged the Best Emerging Author. In 2016, he was listed as one of the top ten most influential authors in India. In 2018, he was awarded by the Young Author Awards in Dubai. Tiwari is the first Indian author to write about sibling relationships in his previous book *Give Your Heart a Break*.

Barabanki is Tiwari's first crime thriller.

Instagram: anujtiwariofficial
Facebook: www.facebook.com/anujtiwari.official
Email: anujtiwari.official@gmail.com
Twitter: @AnujOfficial

Other bestsellers by Anuj Tiwari

It Had To Be You
It's Not Right...But It's Okay
I Tagged Her in My Heart
Give Your Heart a Break

BARABANKI
The Professor, the Pandit and the Policeman

ANUJ TIWARI

Published by
Rupa Publications India Pvt. Ltd 2022
7/16, Ansari Road, Daryaganj
New Delhi 110002

Sales centres:
Allahabad Bengaluru Chennai
Hyderabad Jaipur Kathmandu
Kolkata Mumbai

Copyright © Anuj Tiwari 2022

This is a work of fiction. Names, characters, places and incidents are either the product of the author's imagination or are used fictitiously and any resemblance to any actual person, living or dead, events or locales is entirely coincidental.

All rights reserved.
No part of this publication may be reproduced, transmitted, or stored in a retrieval system, in any form or by any means, electronic, mechanical, photocopying, recording or otherwise, without the prior permission of the publisher.

P-ISBN: 978-93-5520-863-7
E-ISBN: 978-93-5520-864-4

First impression 2022

10 9 8 7 6 5 4 3 2 1

The moral right of the author has been asserted.

Printed in India

This book is sold subject to the condition that it shall not, by way of trade or otherwise, be lent, resold, hired out, or otherwise circulated, without the publisher's prior consent, in any form of binding or cover other than that in which it is published.

To
My daughter, Anvika

Prologue

19 December 2021

Breaking News!

Once called Parijat, the city of Barabanki has become infamous as a hub of illegal drug businesses and crimes in recent times. Counterfeit medicines are manufactured here and supplied not just in the surrounding areas but across the country.

On Saturday, the Uttar Pradesh Special Task Force (UP STF), in a joint operation with Food Safety and Drug Administration (FSDA), recovered a stock of fake antacid syrup and other counterfeit medicines worth ₹15 crore in Barabanki. This stash is associated with the Lucknow pharmaceuticals firm owner Dinesh Agarwal, who was arrested recently. The STF is carrying out further raids to arrest the people whose names have surfaced during the investigation.

The Opposition has asked for the resignation of the chief minister (CM) of Uttar Pradesh, Shri Shiv Narayan, and appealed to the prime minister for a CBI investigation. The media has taken up the story, which may not be a good sign for the ruling party for the next election in 2024.

Moreover, the Uttar Pradesh Legislative Assembly elections is due to be held in the coming few months. Is this a time for the CM to prove his power once again, or is this an alarm bell for the party?

CM Shri Shiv Narayan has asked the Uttar Pradesh Police to start the investigation immediately and submit a weekly report. There was also a late-night meeting at the CM's residence yesterday, where officers of the UP Police were present.

Given the enthusiasm of the current CM, is this a countdown for the elimination of criminals and antisocial elements in Uttar Pradesh? Or will the most significant state in India remain in the business of illegal drugs in the land of Lord Ram?

one

10 January 2022. 10.00 a.m.

The hallway has as much personality as the rest of the hospital. The floor is slate grey and the walls, dove. The ceiling is made of polystyrene squares laid on a grid-like frame. The walls were grey when he visited a few weeks ago. They have been recently painted, unlike his police station.

There are commercial prints on the wall, tasteful but dull. Above every door he passes is a large plastic sign, dark with white lettering—no fancy fonts, just bold and all-caps. His eyes fall on the nameplate declaring the name of a physiotherapist who seems to have been recently appointed, judging from the fresh colour of the nameplate and the new diagrams of the human spine.

Naveen strides ahead, knowing exactly how many steps he needs to take from the reception, which is located in the centre of the hallway, to the chamber he is visiting. The nameplate at the door is written in the same font and colour: 'Dr Shaina'. In a smaller font, probably size 14, Times New Roman, is written 'MBBS, MD'.

Naveen scans the door opposite this chamber. This doctor's nameplate has a different font—it must be size 13, Calibri. This difference irks him so much that he stands frozen at the door for a couple of minutes, unable to move.

With a conscious effort to distract himself, Naveen imagines the doctor's desk, what's kept on the table—on the right, on the left—and what's hanging on the front wall. A picture of a baby comes to mind, which does not make sense at all.

He pauses, tries to see inside the doctor's cabin through the narrow frosted strip-coated glass wall. He rubs his fingers over the coating—it's smooth and strong. Are these strips made of synthetic polymers of polystyrene or polypropylene? Or maybe it's something else.

'Sir, this way,' a nurse says, smiling at him. She points towards the reception.

The TV in the hallway is blasting the breaking news about the recent arrest of a gangster. He feels disappointed about not being a part of the team formed for the investigation of the fake medicine racket that has been running in Uttar Pradesh for the last several years. From the time he has assumed his position as Superintendent of Police (SP), Lucknow, he has always been given cases that only require formalities to be performed.

Twenty-seven-year old IPS officer Naveen Mishra, recruited under UPSC rank 201, is tall, handsome and one of the brightest in his batch. He has all the qualities of the perfect police officer—good knowledge of the law, a strong sense of justice, enthusiasm for action and expert communication skills, whether with other officers or criminals. The ability to think laterally rather than in binaries is what makes Naveen stand out.

However, every character has a flaw. Naveen has OCD, and his recurring anxiety troubles him at times and forces him to pause, even when he is willing to work more.

Naveen takes his cellphone out of his pocket and approaches the nurse's station.

After checking briefly on the system, the nurse tells him, 'Your token number is 7. Token 6 is in progress. Please wait.' She then gives him a fake smile.

Naveen counts the number of files kept on her desk. They must be all for appointments scheduled for today, and the clinic will remain open for new patients for two more hours. That means the number of files divided by the time remaining will be the amount of time the doctor spends with each patient. He calculates 17 minutes, roughly, for each patient. If he's right, the doctor will take 17 minutes more.

'Sure. Thank you,' he tells the nurse and returns to the couch.

Like everything else in the hallway, the couch also tells a story about the personality of the place. It is a piece made more for comfort than style, and must be a moderately priced copy of the work of some truly talented designer. But he starts feeling uncomfortable because of the smell of different chemicals.

'Hello,' Naveen greets the woman sitting opposite him, also waiting.

'Hi,' she responds with a friendly expression.

'I wanted to know, are you not feeling uncomfortable with the smell?'

'Pardon?' she looks confused.

'Nothing. I am good.'

'Are you okay?' she asks.

'Yes, yes, I am fine. Maybe it's just these freshly painted walls that are irritating me.'

'There is no smell from the wall,' she assures him and adds, 'I just visited last week. The walls look the same as now. Are you okay? If you want to go before me, you can go.'

'No, I'm good. I'll just grab some water.'

'Sure.'

Naveen gets up and walks towards the window for some fresh air. He prefers to meet his doctor, even though he usually has to wait to get an appointment.

∞

Thirty minutes have passed when another nurse passes by and says, 'Sir, you are next.'

'Thank you.'

Naveen opens the notepad app in his cellphone and checks the points he wrote yesterday for the appointment. He prefers to be prepared for everything, whether planned or unplanned.

As he walks into the doctor's chamber, Dr Shaina's face cracks into a wide grin, as if greeting an old friend.

He observes her desk and the number of files on it. He wonders how many other patients have seen this smile, and feels the relief they must have felt when they came here. He hopes he feels the same himself.

Dr Shaina completed her studies in the US before settling down to practise here in Lucknow. She has the lithe movement of an athlete and an easy smile. She speaks with an American-Indian accent. But that is not the reason people are waiting to consult her. Her specialization as a psychiatrist and psychologist is what brings people to her. Naveen looks at a frame hanging behind her chair—a certificate from the American Board of Psychiatry and Neurology. Naveen is a dear friend of hers from school.

'Hello, Naveen, how are you?'

Naveen nods, 'I am fine.'

Naveen is pleased to see the silver hair on the doctor. She has a face like some girl you'd ask for directions in the street—non-threatening, lovable. Her hair is tied low in a ponytail.

'So, how many things did you notice while you were waiting outside, which you think others did not?' she asks.

'Come on, I am a police officer and it's my duty to observe things. Not just a hobby. By the way, why do two nameplates in the same hospital on the same floor have different fonts? There must be some logic behind it,' Naveen responds.

Dr Shaina smiles, 'There is no logic behind it. It was not supposed to be this way. They just made a mistake. It will be corrected soon.' She continues, 'So, how are you doing? Is there any progress from the last time we met?'

'I don't think I have any problem or anything that is impacting my work,' Naveen answers. There is certainty in his voice.

'Then why are you here?'

'Because you need a patient.'

'Seriously?' Dr Shaina looks at him questioningly.

'I got a call from Richa, Naveen,' Dr Shaina informs Naveen about the call from his girlfriend, Richa, who is currently in the US completing her studies.

'Why did she call? This is the problem with having a family doctor,' Naveen says and looks at her in an awkward manner.

'She was telling me about your behavioural changes. Also that you unnecessarily think a lot. She mentioned that you are unable to sleep,' Dr Shaina says and waits for him to respond.

'I seriously have no problem. Everyone has anxiety and depression these days because of our lifestyle. Yeah, I get some panic attacks sometimes, and I also feel anxious at work sometimes, but so what?'

'But you are too young to have this, and that is the reason you are here. Naveen, why do you think too much about things?' she asks him.

'I don't know. Maybe I am unable to ignore what I see.'

'Naveen, you are a police officer. I wish I could show you the number of people from the police department who come here for treatment. This is not new to me. Anyway, I'll run some tests for you,' she says, looking him in the eyes with a smile.

She continues, 'Let me ask you something. Do you know that there is a bed inside, and for the last few days, I have been thinking of taking it out and putting in a new one, but I am unable to do that?'

'You are a doctor. You can ask anyone for help and they would do it for you. Even I can do it for you,' Naveen smirks.

'Yes, that's what I want to tell you. When you think some things are not in your control, things that you can't do alone, you call for help. And in your case, I am your help, but you have to promise yourself that you are going to religiously follow what I say.'

He nods.

'Create an album in your imagination. Only add your favourite feel-good moments, and the next time you feel an anxiety attack coming, let the pictures transport you to those times. Also, the good thing about you is, Naveen, you know that you have anxiety. At the same time, you observe things at a very detailed level, even things that may not need your attention. These things make it easier for you to overcome this problem than most people out there. Don't forget that you are a police officer. So, use that strength to find the solution. I am sure you are already doing it.'

'Yeah, yeah, I know. I was treated for anxiety during my preparations for UPSC and then during my training at the Police Academy,' Naveen says.

'Okay, so let's understand it this way. Imagine your brain is a balloon. Six years back, you left a tiny part of your anxiety in it. When you blow the balloon, that tiny particle of anxiety becomes bigger and more visible. That's what is happening with you. So, the simple way to treat that is with medication and meditation. We'll start with this.'

'With me?'

'I am just prescribing some medications. These are regular vitamins that your body needs. And, most importantly, take a break, go on a holiday, alone or with a group, whatever works. But go! You have achieved a lot that few people achieve even after a lot hard work. So, take some time off if you can. And don't stop the meditation.'

'I'm doing that, and it helps,' Naveen says.

'And don't worry, we are sharing things with each other, which is half the win,' the doctor slides his file towards him.

'I agree. Thank you,' Naveen takes the file and gets up from his chair to leave.

When he reaches to open the door, he turns and asks randomly, 'Did you have 13 patients today before me?'

She smiles, 'Including you, yes.'

'Okay. I'll get better soon,' Naveen says, satisfied with the calculation he did while sitting outside.

'Send my regards to Richa. You are lucky to have her. When is she returning from the US?'

'Officially, next year, after completing her MS, but she is coming for a break in a few weeks. I'll give her your regards,' Naveen smiles and leaves.

two

10 January 2022. 3.00 p.m.

'In a dog-eat-dog world, expect to get mugged. Every murderer has a story to tell. A murderer can be a person who killed in self-defense, all the way down to one who kills for fun or greed. Motivation matters very much, Awasthi. One is acting from a sense of love; the other is indifferent and cruel. These are very different personalities and should result in very different responses from society,' Naveen says.

It's a cold winter afternoon. On NH27, with an average speed of a UP Police patrolling van, SP Naveen Mishra and Sub-Inspector R.K. Awasthi are on patrol duty. Looking into the tiny rear-view mirror of the vehicle, Awasthi snaps open the second button of his khaki uniform and adjusts his official shoulder pin. He then proceeds to remove his cap from his head and loosens his old black shoes a bit.

'That's true, sir. Every murderer has a story to tell. Sir, excuse my presumption, but I wanted to ask, is there no chance of your staying here in Lucknow even after promotion?' Awasthi asks. He has recently come to know that Naveen may soon get transferred to Bareilly or Noida.

'There could be a chance if I was a part of the drug racket investigation.'

'Sir, that area comes under our police station, but still we are not a part of it,' Awasthi says, sounding dejected.

'Awasthi! Before joining the police department, my family wanted to make me a doctor, so I took up medicine and even studied it for a year. I left because I wanted to become a police officer. But when I was studying medicine, I came across one famous quote by Carl Jung: "Medicines cure diseases, but only doctors can cure patients." They must be more experienced at solving the case quickly, but I know they will need us at some point of time. So, let's be patient. Somewhere a criminal is waiting for you and me.' Naveen grins at him.

'Sir, experience they may have, but rest, I disagree. The whole department knows you because of your skills. Is it because of Satyendra Verma?' Awasthi asks. He is curious about the rumoured rivalry between Naveen and Verma.

'Who else? I don't know what problem he has with me. That too from the first day. I am half his age!'

'That's the problem. He has been in Lucknow for several years now, and to protect his place, he drags others down. Sir, why don't you talk to him and ask him what the problem is. Why does he always interfere?'

'Awasthi! I can talk to you because you are my friend, but Verma is not a friend. I am UPSC rank 201. I'll handle that motherfucker.'

'I am sure, you will... Sir, UPSC is very difficult, isn't it?'

Naveen starts laughing. 'Anyway, I'll miss your stories when I am transferred, Awasthi. Because of our profession, we can't make many friends outside family. There are only a few I have made in my life.'

'I'll miss you too, sir,' Awasthi smiles at him and continues, 'I have learnt good English with you.'

'Awasthi, use decent instead of good. Times have changed,' Naveen says with a chuckle.

Naveen and Awasthi have been working together for the last three years. They have become good friends, and they know they can depend on each other even in life-threatening situations.

On the law and order front, Uttar Pradesh inherited a helpless police department. The places that should have been 'safe' zones were the 'safari' zones of criminals. For better policing, 41 new police stations and 13 new checkposts were established in the state and 1.37 lakh police personnel were recruited. The government tried hard to bring the law and order situation back on track. As a result, today, either the criminals are fleeing the state or are in prison. However, there are always exceptions, which are never shown on the TV channels or shared with the people. Naveen Mishra is the victim of one such slip. He lost his sister—a victim of domestic violence. He joined the police force many years after this incident.

'Sir, there is one thing that we cannot ignore,' says Awasthi.

'What, Awasthi?' Shifting around to get comfortable, Naveen grunts as the vehicle hits a bump while passing through the Lucknow–Faizabad road.

'By adopting a policy of zero tolerance towards crime and corruption, the police system has been immensely improved. Crime figures have dropped by a considerable extent, but what we see on news channels is confusing, isn't it, sir?'

Naveen leans in his seat and responds, 'Awasthi, figures can be manipulated any time. I don't watch news on the TV. You know why crickets do not sing in winters? Because they prefer warm weather. The warmer it is, the more crickets will sing. When the temperature falls, crickets usually won't sing at all. Our media is just like crickets. When the issue is religion, they will start debating on anything and everything possible. Like emotions sell in Bollywood, religion sells the most in politics. And you don't worry. I still have a month to go, and whoever will come in my place will be a good officer. I'll find out and let you know who is coming if you are worried about who will answer your questions.'

'Sir, so, how has your experience been in Lucknow?' Awasthi asks.

'What do you think, Awasthi, how has my experience been with you over the years?' He winks. 'You know, some say there are good cops and bad cops. But I think that's an oversimplification. They can be honest, courageous, corrupt, devious, malicious, kind or cunning, all at the same time. I have been faithful to my duty first more than anything else from the very first day at the academy. Nothing makes any sense if you cannot offer peace to people.'

After a pause, Naveen asks, 'So, what are your plans for the leave you've taken? Are you taking your family to their grandparents' place?'

'Sir, it is our anniversary, and Mrs Awasthi wishes to have a necklace, but the kids want to go on a vacation. I have to find a midway solution.'

'Then Awasthi, tell Bhabhi ji to take the kids on vacation, and you buy a necklace for her,' says Naveen with a grin.

Awasthi laughs aloud, 'You bet.'

'What?' a surprised Naveen asks and continues, 'What did you say?'

'You bet. My son says this a lot.'

They both laugh.

∞

The weather is gorgeous. There is sweetness in the air that resonates within and finds a way to express this energy in nature. The golden sun paints the evening sky into a bright blue. The blue and red siren lights of the police vehicle are little more than smudgy illuminations in the slanting light of the setting winter sun. But beneath their glow is the white bodywork of a police car. Its yellow-white headlights light up the dense hedgerow to the side of the lane.

'Do you know, sir, Aswathama is still alive?' Awasthi asks.

'Yes, I just saw him yesterday,' Naveen responds.

'No, sir, I am not joking.'

Naveen laughs, 'Okay. Then?'

'So, you must be knowing that Aswathama was a great warrior. He had 64 types of skills and 18 vidyas—different branches of knowledge. He also had a mani, a blessed gem, on his forehead. Draupadi removed this holy mani from his forehead in exchange of forgiving him for killing her sons. I have heard that Aswathama is seen by many people at night-time.'

Naveen starts laughing. 'Awasthi! Really? In real life, there is no Aswathama,' he says.

'I am not joking, sir. People in my village say that he roams around in the night and asks for makhan so that he can apply it on his forehead to get some relief from his wounds,' Awasthi explains.

The police van passes by a congregation. A guruji is addressing a large group of people, just off the road. Awasthi wants to stop for some time and enjoy the prasad, so he says, 'Sir, let's stop for a moment and eat something. We can then directly go back to the police station.'

'Okay, I need to eat something and then have to take these,' Naveen murmurs and keeps the medicines prescribed by Dr Shaina on the dashboard. He stops the vehicle on side of the road.

'Sir, I'll park,' Awasthi takes the keys and leaves to park the car while Naveen takes a walk around the gathering.

'Sir, you should listen to him sometime,' Awasthi says, joining him, as he pours some water from a bottle and washes his hands, spitting out tobacco in the corner.

'We live in a time when we are in a crisis of listeners. We all want to speak more than we want to listen and understand, isn't it? Let's go! Let's listen to him!'

He takes his small baton and walks towards the gathering. They sit in the last row so that they can see when the prasad distribution starts.

The guruji is in the middle of his discourse: 'You know giraffes once had short necks that got progressively longer as members of each subsequent generation stretched their necks as far as they could. And they became the tallest among all but that did not make them the king of the jungle. The lion is always the king of the jungle. So, balance is always necessary, and if someone tries to disrupt the balance, you should speak up. One fundamental principle of religion is the idea that people's actions and thoughts directly determine their current life and future lives. We all are blessed to be born in Hindu culture, and you must protect your religion and culture like a lion. There are giraffes with growing population.'

'Did Guruji join a political party or what?' Naveen whispers sarcastically.

'Seems like. He is clearly referring to those who live in old Lucknow and near Hussainabad area when he talks about giraffes. Anyway, he is strongly supporting the party in the upcoming legislative assembly election.'

'Behenchod! Everyone in Uttar Pradesh is either a politician or dreams of becoming one. Look at these kids. They don't know what they are learning.' Naveen sounds frustrated. 'Awasthi, where have you been posted for elections duty?' he continues.

'Sir, what to say, they have sent me to the outskirts of Barabanki area, and there is a different case going on there...'

Naveen laughs, 'What happened, Awasthi? You always have a story to share.'

'Sir, I am not joking. The Election Commission has given an election symbol of typewriter. Now, in the village, no one has ever seen a typewriter in their lives. Some see it as snake, some see it as kite, while others see it as telephone. Except typewriter, they see everything. The candidate's family members are protesting against the Election Commission.'

Naveen starts laughing, 'This is news!'

'Sir, by the way, you have to go to an annual ceremony of the City Montessori School as a chief guest, no?' Awasthi reminds him.

'Yes, at 7.00 p.m. And you are also coming with me,' Naveen says.

'You are the chief guest, sir. What will I do there?' responds Awasthi.

'Then you come as a chief guest, I'll join you as your friend, sounds good?' Naveen shrugs.

'Sir...' Awasthi smiles at him and adds, 'Okay, sir, I'll come with you.' He appreciates the invitation. 'Sir, when is your cousin coming to Lucknow? You were telling the other day. You both have to come home for dinner or lunch, whatever suits you.'

'Yeah, Raghav! He is coming next week. He has asked me to take a day off. Let's see.' And that reminds Naveen to drop Raghav a text to confirm his arrival.

The walkie-talkie beeps: 'This is Munshi Pulia Police Chowki. Munshi Pulia Police Chowki, there is a report from IEC College, near Green City petrol pump. There is an emergency, please report it—Dullapur, near Indian Oil petrol pump. Please respond.'

Awasthi picks up the walkie-talkie and responds, 'Duty vehicle is on the way. Duty vehicle is on the way.' 'I had to reach home early,' he murmurs in disappointment.

'Awasthi, how come you have forgotten? This is the birthplace of Kunti, so how you can expect the day to end without a Mahabharata unfolding, as you say. Let's go!' Naveen and Awasthi get up and approach the vehicle.

'True, sir. Sir, we'll eat something on the way.'

'Sure.'

'Did you get the approval to install a small TV in the patrolling van?' Awasthi asks and adds, 'Like these days, all cabs have it.'

Naveen starts laughing, 'Awasthi! We'll get one in this van? You are so funny.'

'Sir, I'll drive,' Awasthi says, and they leave.

∞

'Sir, tell me one thing,' Awasthi asks while driving.

'Yes, Awasthi.'

'Sir, does it not bother you ever when you chase a criminal between life and death?'

Naveen laughs. 'Awasthi, we have not seen our soldiers fight the war. When you are facing the enemies, and the sound of every bullet passes through your ears as if in Dolby surround sound, you forget life and death. In that moment, you have just one duty—to kill the enemies and come out safely. There is no second thought. My brother used to tell me how he fought against enemies. He always said that there is nothing like being an army officer. He used to tell me, "Naveen, when I wear the uniform, I forget everything. There is nothing else required to purify my soul."'

'So…'

'He was martyred two years ago in Pathankot. Forget it! What were you saying…oh yeah, if I have the fear of getting killed or not. Awasthi, when the criminals are using guns, the police must carry weapons too. After that, the death count is a matter of time and is doomed to escalate. When a bullet is fired at you, you must pick one and pull the trigger or run.'

'I get it.'

Awasthi drives the vehicle through a shortcut, more of a dirt track that has been hacked out of the wheat fields, barely wide enough for the van. They screech down the slope of Dullapur. The vehicle takes a shower of dirt and then suddenly everything becomes clearer just when they take a left turn towards the college gate. The gates are already open. It looks like there is extra security at the entry.

With a shriek of the siren, the police van enters the scene. Everyone clears the path till the vehicle stops in front of the hostel. Awasthi calls for a status report on the radio and gets out of the vehicle. SP Naveen Mishra opens the door and gets down. He is the very epitome of authority, with his gun hanging idly at his hip. Naveen sees a man sitting on the bench at the entrance of the hostel. He beckons him while looking around the 15-floor hostel.

Right in front of the building, a body is lying on the ground in a pool of blood emerging from the head. The boy has clearly fallen from one of the upper floors of the hostel building and seems to have been gravely injured.

'Did you call the police?' Awasthi asks the warden of the hostel, who was sitting on the bench outside. He puts up a barrier around the body to prevent anyone from entering.

'Yes, sir,' the lean man says as he approaches the police officer, almost shaking. He points up at the building and murmurs, 'I saw him just yesterday. He was fine.'

Naveen approaches the body and shouts, 'Awasthi, call the ambulance, right now, we'll need to take him to the hospital.'

'Yes, sir.'

One of the students comes up to the policemen. 'Sir, I know him. Not just me. The whole college knows him. He was the general secretary of the youth club. He was placed in an MNC just last semester, so everybody was talking about him. When I came here, he was not conscious,' he said.

'Who is he?' Awasthi questions.

'I am from first year, civil engineering. I found the body...'

'I am not asking your introduction, Obama ji, what's his name?' Awasthi points towards the body.

'Sir, Ajay Nagar...'

Before the student says anything further, Awasthi pushes him aside, saying, '...you concentrate on your studies and find a solution to how you can make this country free of potholes and don't become Sherlock Holmes. Go!'

The DCP's van reaches the place. Just then, Ajay's father comes running towards them. Tears well up in his eyes as he sees the still body of his son lying on the ground.

Naveen crouches to examine the body closely. His neck and shoulder have marks on them. He brings his fingers close to his nostrils to check if he is still alive. There is blood everywhere, blood on his kurta, blood on his face. He is dead.

'Where is the ambulance, Awasthi?' Naveen shouts and his voice echoes around the hostel. 'Also, Awasthi, I need still and video photography to record the crime scene from every angle and every elevation available,' commands Naveen.

'Okay, sir,' confirms Awasthi.

Naveen takes the handkerchief out of his pocket and picks up the cigarette lying near the body. 'Awasthi! I need the forensic team now and make sure no one enters this place without my permission.'

'Sure, sir.'

As Naveen looks at the students standing around, he suddenly spots his cousin Raghav, who is standing with a girl a few feet away. As he stares at them, the girl pulls out her phone and clicks a picture, she then heads towards the exit.

Raghav is an alumnus of IEC, and he is now a writer.

He has been invited to IEC to conduct a paid workshop. He was the secretary of the youth club in his last year of college. Naveen is shocked to see Raghav in the college, since he was expecting him to arrive much later, and Raghav hadn't told him of any change in plans.

Raghav nods at him.

When DCP Harsh Vardhan sees the girl take the photo, he shouts, 'Stop. No one will take any picture here. Clear this place,' he instructs. The girl shakes her head apologetically. She stays back. She keeps her phone in her pocket.

'Warden, I want to interrogate some of your students,' DCP Harsh Vardhan says, now taking over the investigation.

The warden looks surprised.

'We can record in-person interrogation with the students,' the DCP continues. 'There's no mandate that we need permission, and if we waste time taking permission from your dean to interrogate, we may miss the real cause of the death,' says the officer and adds, 'Awasthi and Naveen, keep an eye on everyone. No one goes out of the college without my permission. Send in all the students who are here now one by one.'

'Yes, sir,' they reply and nod.

The DCP then enters the warden's office adjacent to him to begin the interrogations. He meets a few students before the girl who took the photo is called in. 'What's your name? Sit down,' he says to her.

'Jayanti, sir.'

'I know you're afraid to talk right now, but we need your help,' DCP says.

'I'll help in whatever way I can,' she says, almost whispering. She looks very disturbed.

'Why were you taking pictures?' he asks.

'Ajay and I were a part of the same club, sir. We had organized several events in the college. There is no other reason. When you told us to stop, I did not take the picture. You can check my phone...'

'This is not the right place for taking photos. Do you want to share something with me?'

'Sir, I was feeling breathless, so I was just going out to get some air.'

'And now you are fine?'

She nods.

'You know, Jayanti, I am wondering why you had such a reaction. The other students were also shocked by what happened, but nobody reacted like you.'

'Sir, I already told you, I knew him well. I'll try to help however I can. We have lost a friend. The college has lost a bright student. His family has lost a young child,' she replies, this time much more confident.

The ambulance comes in with aggressive speed, the kind of sheer driving audacity that lets everyone know the siren isn't a polite request to move. Every head turns to follow the yellow and blue streak. Every heart in the college skips a beat. There is something in the intensity of the moment.

Raghav can hear Ajay's father sobbing. All the students present look shocked. A muscle twitches involuntarily at the corner of his right eye; his mouth forms a rigid line.

Raghav approaches Naveen. 'Hello Bhaiya! My workshop date shifted, so I came here earlier than planned. I was going to call you, but I thought I'll finish the workshop here and then meet you.'

'Okay. See you at home in the evening,' Naveen replies.

Raghav walks closer to Naveen and whispers, 'I don't think it's a suicide.' He adds, 'I think he was pushed. It's a parabolic fall, which means someone pushed him. If someone commits suicide, he will never jump like he is diving. He will simply fall to the floor.'

'Hmm, makes sense.'

'Jayanti may have something important to share with you,' Raghav tells Naveen.

Naveen looks around and then takes him to the empty corner of the hostel corridor. 'What do you mean Jayanti has something to share? Regarding this? Where is she?'

'She is there.' Raghav points towards the glass window of the office where the DCP is talking to Jayanti and the warden.

'She is already troubled because of me, please help her, and I don't think she needs to be questioned right now,' Raghav says.

Naveen can see that Raghav is sincere. He is really concerned about Jayanti. So he goes up to the warden's office.

'I am sorry for interrupting, but I need to talk to her urgently,' Naveen looks at Jayanti and then at the DCP.

'What do you mean?' asks the DCP, getting up from the chair.

'I just need her for a moment, please,' says Naveen.

The DCP nods. 'You go,' he tells Jayanti and then calls Raghav through the glass window and asks, 'And you are from which year?'

'I am not from this college.'

'Then what are you doing here and how did you enter the institute?' he asks, raising his brows.

'I am an alumnus, and I have come for a workshop. Also,

I made an entry in the college register at the gate. I came here for Jayanti's well-being,' he answers. Jayanti gets up from her chair. The DCP nods.

'There are some surveillance cameras in the college, right?' the DCP asks the warden who was hovering around.

'Yes, sir,' the warden replies.

'Yes, those might help you in the investigation,' Raghav adds.

'Okay, you can go, but you will not leave the city without our permission. You have to take permission from the police station if there is anything urgent.'

'Sure, sir. I have no plans to leave the city. I need to be with Jayanti,' he smiles and leaves.

'Naveen, make sure nobody goes out without my permission,' announces the DCP.

'Okay, sir,' Naveen responds.

'Also, inform the victim's family members to come to the police station,' adds the DCP.

'Any prima facie?' The DCP asks Naveen.

'Sir, we'll register the FIR and wait for the post-mortem report before we can determine if this is a suicide or a murder. But we'll surely find something,' Awasthi reports to the DCP, as he walks in.

The DCP looks at Naveen and says, 'Naveen, this is your case. Make sure you start work on this ASAP and submit the charge sheet as soon as possible. It is not just about the case anymore, and it is not about the college's reputation. CM sir and Guruji are coming to the college for the inaugural ceremony of the statue of Lord Ram after they address an election rally, the Jan Vishwas Yatra. Before this becomes a political and religious matter in the media, either solve it, or if it gets difficult, better close the file. There will be pressure coming from the top soon. Be prepared for it. I don't want to get transferred to Noida again because if I go, you are coming with me. Let's find the killer and close the case.'

'Yes, sir! No worries, sir. I am on duty and on standby if there is anything required. I'll not disappoint you. I'll be working on this only. Just taking this ahead under 174 CrPC.'

'Good. As soon as you get the post-mortem report, please let me know. Listen! I must leave. Please keep me posted on the progress. And monitor all entry and exit points of the college. Especially that new guy—Raghav. Keep an eye on him, and take a statement from everyone if needed. They are all adults.'

∞

'Naveen sir, I'll get the post-mortem report in a few hours, once I receive it from the mortuary technician,' Awasthi informs Naveen after receiving the confirmation from the mortuary office.

'Great. Send me a copy.'

'Sure, sir.'

'Why don't you come with me?' Naveen asks Raghav.

'Now?' asks Raghav, looking around him awkwardly.

'Feeling awkward to sit in the police vehicle, is it?' asks Naveen as he puts on his sunglasses.

'Nothing like that Bhaiya! Just…'

'No problem, meet me at the college gate then.'

'No, no, I am okay. Should we take Jayanti also?'

'If you are coming for a get-together, then for sure.' Raghav gets the point and does not persist.

'Sir, you sit comfortably, I'll drive,' Awasthi says. Naveen nods, gives him the keys and settles in the passenger seat. Raghav gets in the back of the car as they drive off.

'Awasthi, take a round of the college. DCP sir was asking about the surveillance cameras installed in the college. I want to take the route.'

'Okay, sir,' says Awasthi and drives through the campus, going past the lake inside, the guest house, faculty house and then the laundry area.

'Okay, let's go now,' says Naveen. The sun has touched the horizon.

'Sir, I'll drop you to the office and then I need to go...' Awasthi says.

'Where are you going, Awasthi?' Naveen asks him and adds, 'Did you re-take the statement of the man who first told us about Ajay at the hostel?'

'Yes, sir, I took that. Also, will upload the crime scene sketch in the system and attach a copy in the file in case you need to have a look for further enquiry. Naveen sir, it slipped my mind, but I got a message from the station that I have to go for a court hearing. May I be on my way?' Awasthi requests.

Naveen is concerned. 'Court hearing? Which other cases are you handling, Awasthi? Has Bhabhi ji filed a case against you for not giving her a necklace?'

'Sir, last month, I was on duty with Verma sir. He seized a vehicle that was parked in front of this college only. He then took the seized vehicle to his in-laws. The vehicle owner checked the vehicle's location on his phone and was surprised to see the vehicle moving almost 143 kilometres away from Lucknow, in the Lakhimpur Kheri area. The owner immediately locked his vehicle through the app, using a high-end security feature, which left us stranded midway and stopped the SUV's engine and locked it entirely for two hours. On learning what had happened, Verma sir had to request the vehicle owner several times to unlock the vehicle. Sub Inspector Shukla and I were also with him. I thought it was my last day with Verma sir.' Awasthi sounds helpless while narrating the whole incident.

Naveen starts laughing, 'Seriously, Awasthi? 143 kilometers?'

'Yes, sir, it came in the news also after that. Verma sir was suspended for a couple of days because he was driving the vehicle and enquiry started, so... This would have not been an issue if it had not come on the news. I have been asked to be present for the hearing, so I need to go.'

Naveen is in deep thought. 'Hmm, and you ask me why Satyendra Verma does not like me. Nothing you can do about this. Go!'

'I have nothing to say, Naveen sir. Well, all the best for a lovely evening for your event at the school,' says Awasthi and leaves.

three

10 January 2022. 6:30 p.m.

The walls of the police station are as thick as a medieval castle and the windows almost as mean. There's no flicker of light in some of the lock-ups when the main wooden doors are closed.

Naveen and Raghav are about to leave the police station for the school event when Awasthi enters the police station and approaches Naveen in a hurry.

'What happened, Awasthi? I thought you left for home directly from the court,' says Naveen.

'Sir, the post-mortem report has come over email, so I thought of sharing it with you first. We'll get the physical copy soon,' Awasthi shows the report on his cellphone.

Cause of Death: Head trauma, internal bleeding and complications of a bone fracture.

Note: There is a substantial amount of Calcium Carbonate content found in the body. The substance did not have any effect on the body in the past 48 hours.

Further correlation required.

A dynamic thinker sees the relationships between concepts rather than getting tied into binary thinking. Naveen sees something that may not be completely true but not false either.

Awasthi knows Naveen's expression well. 'What happened, sir?' he asks.

'Nothing. Do we have the sketch of the scene ready?' he asks.

'Yes, sir. Anything suspicious?'

'Too early to say. Give me that sketch.'

Naveen turns towards Raghav. 'You were telling me earlier that it does not look like a suicide...'

'I mean, see where he fell off...' Raghav pitches in.

Awasthi hands Naveen the sketch, 'Sir.'

'Awasthi, if you want to go home, please go. I'm going to take some time. Please forward the port-mortem report to my email,' Naveen keeps the sketch on the table and sits on one side.

'Aren't you coming home for dinner?' Awasthi asks Raghav and then looks at Naveen for approval.

'Some other day. Raghav is here only. We'll come for sure,' he nods and gets back to the sketch.

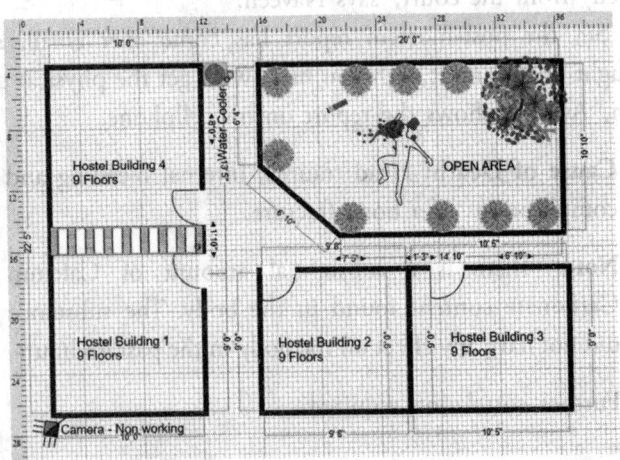

'See, I am sure you have also noticed he fell at least six feet away from the terrace or balcony of the hostel,' Raghav says.

'...and it's hard to believe that he was smoking one moment and decided to commit suicide and jumped off. I am not able to digest this,' Naveen adds. He checks the post-mortem report again and goes through it.

'You have been in college for how many days now?' asks Naveen.

'Three days. Today is the fourth day.'

'Did you notice anything in the college? Any small thing? Anything you noticed in Jayanti maybe? They were in the same club, right?'

'Hmm...nothing as such. I met Jayanti after three years, so just usual talk. I recently came to know that she lost her father a year ago. He was also a police officer but later joined the army. Ansari sir and her father were good friends. Her father was murdered mysteriously, and the killers were never identified. In fact, Jayanti told me that the officer who tried to open the case was transferred a few months ago. She asked me if I could help her get his file, which was closed. So, I was going to ask you if it is possible for her to check the file. I know it's not the protocol, but maybe that's the only way I can help her.'

'When the file is closed, why does she want to have a look? By the way, who is Ansari sir?' Naveen asks him.

'Ansari sir is from the college only. After she lost her father, he was the one who helped her to process her educational loan for the college.'

'Okay. That's nice of him. Well, listen! I want to go to the college again with you,' Naveen says, putting all the papers back in the file and carefully placing it in his drawer.

'I should be the one asking you for help. Not the other way round,' Raghav says sarcastically.

'I don't want to go as a police officer. Just like a common friend of both of you. Because there is one thing bothering me since we exited the college from the other side. There were CCTVs installed, but most of them had a blind spot.'

'How is this suicide or murder related to the CCTVs having a blind spot? And you know how big the institute is, you can't just say anything about it,' Raghav says him. 'I mean, you know the reputation of the college,' Raghav continues, then hesitates.

'What happened?'

'Nothing. I don't know how to share this with you, but something really embarrassing happened.' Raghav does not want anyone to know about this, but he thinks if he shares it with Naveen, he can give him a suggestion like an elder brother in case something goes wrong.

'What happened?'

'Jayanti and I went to the guest house terrace after dinner and someone might have seen us. Jayanti was really upset after this incident.'

'Wait, any idea where would Ajay usually be at this hour in the evening? Anything you knew about him?' asks Naveen.

'I don't know. This morning, we were called to the dean's office, but luckily, it was not about us romancing on the terrace of the guest house,' he answers.

'Did you meet Ajay during your stay here?'

'I met Ajay when I reached college. He was very positive about my arrival, and we were supposed to catch up, but then…'

'Where was Jayanti when you came to know about Ajay's death?' Naveen is trying find a link between all these separate incidents. He takes a print-out of the post-mortem report, takes out the file again and keeps the sketch and a blank sheet of paper on the table. He then draws four circles: one around the additional note that says that there was a substantial amount of chalk-like content in the body. The second circle is around the body in the sketch. And the third circle he makes on the blank paper and writes, 'CCTV'. The last circle he draws in the centre and connects all the other circles to it. He leaves this circle blank.

'What are you trying to link here?' Raghav looks confused. 'Are you suspecting Jayanti by any chance? There are 1,300 students in the college, you know.'

'I am not suspecting anyone for now. But you have to tell me everything from the very first day when you entered the college. I can trust you, and this is completely off the record, but you have to help me. If I am right, I'll be the first one to crack it.'

'I am a writer. My work is only to write stories and not be a part of them.'.

'Don't worry. You can trust me.'

'Okay. But you have to help Jayanti and show her her father's file.'

'Negotiating with a police officer!' Naveen raises his eyebrows. 'Okay, done.'

'Thank you, Bhaiya! I'll tell Jayanti.'

Raghav then starts telling Naveen everything that happened over the last four days, right from when he reached the college.

four

6 January 2022. 10.00 a.m.

A soft sigh escapes Raghav's lips as he shuts his eyes tight, trying to escape the clutches of his painful memories. Last night, Raghav found Jayanti's letter tucked within the pages of his notebook; she wrote it three years ago. He stayed up the whole night pondering the same question that bothered him when he first received the letter: how could someone write a break-up letter that also consoled him? If she cared so much about him, then why did she leave? And if she never cared, then why did she console him before saying goodbye?

It's a cold, moist Monday morning, and Raghav has woken up later than usual. Nervous, he works some more on the first draft he has been working on for so long. Jayanti pops up in his mind again. Nothing can be better than going back to his college as an accomplished and celebrated author now, making Jayanti realize that leaving him was a mistake.

As a writer, Raghav is a modern-day wizard. The right words written can heal the brain, heal a culture and help form reality itself, and Raghav can do all of these. He combines fiction with reality, and this perfect combination makes him India's bestselling author. This is especially remarkable, since he is a trained engineer, an alum of Indian Engineering College (IEC), Lucknow. His first book was about his own love story and the break-up. In it, he tried to answer the question of why Jayanti left him. Why does anybody leave someone in a relationship? Why do we become so helpless in a relationship that we do not have any control over our emotions? The book became a bestseller, and he went on to write many more stories after that. But this has remained the most special to him, and it is the one that is sold and read the most, even after years.

Standing in front of a seven-foot blackwood frame mirror, Raghav stares at his lean frame, fit and muscular from jogging and yoga. His intense brown eyes stare back at him as he takes in the ruffled hair and dark circles.

'Many times, we pretend that we forget the past, but we don't. We just replace it with someone else's presence in life,' he wrote in one of his books. Aren't three years enough to forget someone completely? Has he really forgotten Jayanti? If he has, why does he feel this desperate urge to go back to college? Just to show her how much he has accomplished without her? Maybe that's precisely why he should avoid going there.

Suddenly Siri beeps a reminder, and within a moment, his phone rings. It's Rosaline.

Rosaline has been his publicist for the last few years. She also organizes his events and workshops. Raghav puts the letter back into the notebook and answers the call.

'Hello, Rosaline, how are you doing?' Raghav asks.

'Good morning! I am good, Raghav. Why do you even keep a phone when you don't want to pick up calls?'

'It was on silent,' says Raghav and checks his cellphone. Five missed calls from Rosaline. 'Sorry!'

'That's okay. Are you ready for the workshop in Lucknow? I will have to inform the university officials about your arrival.'

Raghav hesitates for a moment. 'I think I'll skip this. I am not feeling well,' he says.

'Umm, if you are not feeling well, I'll understand. I will let them know that you can't make it this time. But Raghav, anyway, it's going to be three-day workshop. And it's your college! Maybe sometimes it is good to look at the past, just with a new perspective?'

'You can't give me that as a reason to go.'

'No problem, fine. You take care. I'll drop them an email. In case you change your mind, please let me know.'

'Hmm... Okay, I'll manage,' he says. 'I haven't been on a solo trip for a while. This could work as a solo trip.'

'So, you want to go?' asks Rosaline, surprised.

'Yeah,' he says, giving in.

'Anyway, this gig is paying well, and it's your college. They will be happy to see you.'

'Let's see. But please ask them not to arrange accommodation outside the college. I can't waste time travelling around Lucknow. I am okay to stay at the college guest house,' he suggests.

'Roger that,' she replies. 'It's going to be a long day tomorrow, Raghav. Your flight is early in the morning. I have already forwarded you the email. I hope you have all the details. There will be a cab waiting at the airport...'

'Got it.'

'Okay. Just one more thing, just to remind you, you have

that Dubai event coming up next week. That is going to be a big one.'

'I remember. Thanks, Rosaline. You have always been sweeter to me than Siri,' says Raghav and disconnects.

∞

The next morning, after a delayed flight from Mumbai to Lucknow, Raghav gets into the car waiting for him at the Lucknow airport to take him to the college. Situated on the banks of the Gomti River, Lucknow is home to the remains of one of the most sophisticated and celebrated cultures of the Indian subcontinent, the kingdom of Awadh. Raghav has many memories from the four years he spent in the city, and is always excited to visit. Some places stand out, especially Sharma ki Chai, or Shree Lassi at Chowk or Kali Gajar ka Halwa at Akbari Gate. These are tied to unforgettable memories with Jayanti.

Raghav stretches and gazes tiredly out of the window. The closer the cab gets to the college, the colder he feels.

He was the secretary of the youth club in the last year of college. He met Jayanti during the college fest through his friend from first year, Kavya. Jayanti was also in first year, and she was participating in a cultural event. Kavya shared a special bond with Raghav. They got along well, as they were both from the same city of Dehradun, the capital of scenic beauty.

Gradually, Jayanti began to develop feelings for Raghav and eventually confided in him. While the other seniors in college were pretty bossy, Raghav was kind and considerate to his juniors. That was precisely the reason why he was the secretary of the youth club. Raghav wasn't someone with a chiseled jaw or seductive eyes. He was average-looking yet charming. His thoughtful acts, genuineness and kind gestures could easily make anyone fall head over heels in love with him.

Raghav started sharing the same bond with Jayanti that he shared with Kavya. The three became a family away from home in college. They celebrated late-night birthdays, and spent hours over numerous cups of tea on lazy afternoons in the canteen. The evenings would call for aimless strolling under the moonlight within the campus and on the streets of Lucknow, with much laughter and happiness. Dinner was just an excuse to meet everyone at the same table.

During this beautiful journey, love blossomed between Raghav and Jayanti, and very dramatically, Jayanti proposed to Raghav on his birthday in the library. Many girls were after Raghav, but he was waiting for this day—he wanted Jayanti too.

They were madly in love, and within no time, they became the most popular couple in college. Love—the foundation of every problem and, sometimes, the solution too.

However, they were dreading the future: in a couple of months, Raghav was going to leave college. They were both scared about whether long distance would work, and so they stopped sharing their fears of being apart and became possessive. This led to fights and arguments. Even though they both tried to make the relationship last, something or the other happened that affected their relationship. That was the year when their relationship suffered the most, and promises made in winter were broken in summer.

Raghav searches for the letter in his backpack. A mere sheet of paper that holds power to tear his heart apart every time he reads it.

Hi Raghav,

This isn't working, Raghav. You know why I agreed on a date tonight? Honestly, because I thought you may have planned a surprise for me. A perfect romantic date. But you didn't even come close. When you walked out to attend a call, my stupid heart still believed you'd possibly come back with a little ring or probably just a little something to keep the adrenaline going, but much to my disappointment, it was all in vain. Silly me! Sometimes we break our own hearts through stupid expectations. We're probably better off without each other. It'll possibly do us good to part ways. Better to have two happy homes than one sad home, Raghav. And there is a lot I want to write, but you hate reading long letters. Please take care. Goodbye.

Jayanti

The driver breaks Raghav's reverie. He asks, 'Sir, you are a writer?'

'Yes,' Raghav nods. 'You are from the college?'

'Yes. I have been working for the college for more than 10 years now. We never seem to have met in college,' he says. The driver seems keen to chat, 'I am originally from Faizabad, but I work here.' He continues, 'Sir, you are actually a writer, I mean, one who writes a full book?'

Raghav laughs, 'Yes, I am a writer.'

'Sir, you are Raghav Sharma?'

'Yes,' replies Raghav.

'Sir, now I know, there are hoardings in college. Some students were talking about you. We are so happy that from our college, you have achieved so much. You even live in Mumbai now. It's not easy to write a book. Sir, how many books have you written?'

'Six.'

'Oh, six books. You are the Virat Kohli of our IEC,' he says with a wide smile.

'Thank you,' Raghav shakes his head with the tiniest of smiles.

'And here we are.'

The cab drifts smoothly to the left, stopping in front of the big gate displaying the words 'Indian Engineering College'.

'Sir, we have reached.' The driver says looking back at him with affection and respect.

Raghav peeps out of the window. It's been three years since he left this college. He sets his hair and licks his lips to make them look fresh and lively, which he thinks is a natural and instant make-up tool for guys. Unfortunately, he can't pinch his cheeks in public to make them blush.

The two giant iron gates open for the car, and they make their way down the concrete driveway lined with trees.

When they stop, a short boy in a brown jacket comes forward and holds the door open. 'Hello, sir, hope you are doing well?' asks the boy.

Another student arrives behind the first and says, 'Welcome, sir.'

'I am good. How are you guys doing?' Raghav responds, smiling at the students standing around him.

Wearing shorts and a t-shirt was a bad idea, especially in the month of January when the college is wrapped in fog.

Raghav notices a student who was in Jayanti's batch, Ajay, standing a few steps away near the security guard's office.

'Hello, Ajay,' Raghav calls out to him.

Ajay turns back and says with a smile, 'Hello Raghav sir. Welcome back to your own college after years. We've waited so long for you to visit.'

Raghav shrugs and nods, 'I could not come for the convocation, so I thought of coming for the workshop. How are you doing?'

'I am good. Guys, take him to the guest house,' says Ajay looking at the juniors who are excitedly waiting around.

'Sure, sir,' all three respond in sync.

'See you around. I just need to rush for something urgent. Let's catch up when your schedule permits,' says Ajay.

'Yeah, see you at the workshop this afternoon,' responds Raghav with a grin.

'Sure, sure,' Ajay waves and heads towards the main gate.

Technically, Ajay and Raghav have a senior–junior relationship, but they have played a lot of matches of cricket together for the college, and such a relationship survives even after years.

They walk towards the guest house, situated behind the faculty house, following the shortest path.

Raghav observes the lake while crossing the basketball court, and then in a split second, he feels the cold chill and air gusts.

'Hope you enjoy your time here,' Sudeep, one of the three students, says.

'I'm sure I will.'

'Yes, sir.'

'Things have changed here. You have surveillance cameras in the college now,' Raghav says as he takes his cellphone out from his pocket and to inform Rosaline about his arrival.

'Yes, sir. Couples used to sit here in the park, so the college has installed a few cameras here. They are also planning to put more in the next few months across hostels and the academic block to avoid ragging.'

'Really? Will it work, though? Because they are not aligned. These are fixed cameras, and between every two cameras, there is a blind spot,' he says. He adds, 'And, you know, most of the accidents happen in the blind spots.'

'A girl went to the boys' hostel recently, and the rumour got spread that she got pregnant, so they have become stricter now.'

'That's funny.'

Sudeep asks politely, 'Sir, are you a friend of Jayanti ma'am from the fourth year?'

'I am an alumnus of this college, batch 2007–11,' Raghav responds, trying to avert the unexpected question about Jayanti.

'Actually, she only referred your name to the dean, so I thought you are ma'am's friend. But we are so glad that you are here,' he says. They then reach the guest house, where four students are waiting to welcome him with a bouquet.

five

7 January 2022. 11.00 a.m.

After speaking at more than a hundred events, Raghav has realized that the nervousness of the first day is there to protect him, as if those feelings are asking him to check for traffic before crossing the road. As he enters the academic zone of the institute, his senses are heightened.

He notices the familiar shoes first—the leather belly shoes he was so very familiar with. He slows down and looks up. Jayanti still walks with her shoulders drawn back. Her eyes are on the notebook in her hand. She hasn't noticed him because he's behind her. However, when they reach the end of the corridor, she turns and bumps into Raghav.

Jayanti, 22, 5'2, looks beautiful in the college uniform. Her innocent yet playful eyes, long eyelashes and pronounced cheekbones are framed by her kohl-black hair, which plunges over her shoulders. Her understated beauty makes Raghav go weak in the knees. Her enticing constellation-black eyes holds him captive in her gaze.

'Hi, how are you? How come you are here?' asks Jayanti.

Is she not aware about his arrival? What about the banners in the college? What about the conversation he had with the student this morning about how she recommended him? These questions instantly dart through his mind. Raghav feels slightly annoyed. He points towards the banner at the entrance of the academic block just behind them, and says, 'I am doing well and I hope you are doing well too, as you always did. I thought you knew about it. These posters? They are not fake, are they? I have been invited for a workshop.'

'Oh, I did not know. Well, all the best for the workshop,' responds Jayanti, with a neutral expression.

'That's okay, thanks.'

She nods and walks off to the right, while Raghav takes the left towards the auditorium. He wonders while entering the auditorium how did she not know about the workshop, and if indeed she did know, why did she lie about it? He turns, and looking at her receding form, murmurs, 'How can someone be so ruthless even after so many years…'

As he gazes at her, Jayanti stumbles on the staircase. He instinctively takes a step towards her but then changes his mind and turns to enter the auditorium.

'Hello, Ansari sir, how are you?' Raghav greets the professor who seems to be waiting for someone in the corridor.

'I am good. How are you doing? You have become an influential famous personality. Isn't it? I follow you on Instagram,' Professor Ansari responds.

'I am fine. I feel blessed to come back here again. Thank you for following me. I just post regular content.'

'Are you happy to visit your college again?'

'Yes, of course. Are you waiting for someone? Or are you

joining us in the workshop?' Raghav asks, curious.

'No, no, I was just waiting for you.'

'For me? Anything you wanted to talk about, sir?' Raghav is surprised.

Professor Ansari says, 'You are an influential person. Or what is it called in your language, influencer. You are an influencer, and people listen to your words and follow you. I can only teach people, but you can change their minds.'

Raghav is confused. 'I understand, sir, but what did you want to talk about?'

'The truth. How our community is suffering and struggling. Hindus are torturing us. Political parties look at us only as a vote bank and then cast us aside. They took the mosque also from us. No Hindu spoke against it. We need some people like you from your community to help us and encourage equality.'

'Equality? What equality are you talking about? The only recent news I heard about your community was about love jihad.'

'No, no, that is not true. The media, these politicians, they just spread false news. It's all just negative propaganda, not the truth. Whatever you are reading in newspapers these days is complete bullshit. If a Hindu girl loves a Muslim boy and marries him, what is wrong with that?'

'There is nothing wrong if that love isn't motivated by religion.'

'This is just love between two people.'

'Sure. I would love to talk to your more, but the workshop will begin soon.'

'May Allah bless you with prosperity. You can come home anytime. I live in the faculty house, just opposite the guest house.'

'Thank you, sir,' says Raghav.

'What happened, Raghav?' Professor Ansari places a hand on his shoulder.

'Nothing, I am fine,' he takes a deep breath, trying to calm his mind.

'Tell me what you're thinking,' he insists.

'Before I leave, I would like to say that you have been a great teacher of chemistry in this college and your contribution to the youth club is immense. I have immense respect for you, but the brain uses the same equipment for love and hate, as per my understanding. If you are expecting me to speak for you without knowing anything about your problems or your opinions, I don't think I can do it. I am not against any community, but whenever it is needed, I'll stand by the truth, no matter what it takes.'

Professor Ansari nods.

'Also, sir, not everything in the media is fake or false. There is always a truth that intellectual people like you and I know, not the common people. I'll see you around.'

∞

As it's the first day of the workshop, Raghav feels energetic and is meticulously prepared. He takes four stairs to reach the podium, from where he can see everyone. He rolls up his sleeves and takes a sip of water before he begins. He is wearing blue jeans with a white cotton shirt and a blue jacket. A turquoise muffler around his neck adds to his personality.

Raghav takes in the students seated around the auditorium, with a semi-circular seating arrangement, inspired by historic Greek amphitheaters. He notices Jayanti in the audience in the last row but decides not to look at her.

He begins with sharing his journey so far, which creates an atmosphere of trust, eliminating the formality between the audience and him.

Then he goes on, 'A time comes when you try hard to fix things in life, and then there comes a time when everything breaks, leaving you hopeless and dejected—broken, beyond repair. At that moment, you will have two thoughts: "I want to jump from the cliff and not face the world", or "I am now free to let myself start afresh". Usually, we go with the first option. But still, you have a choice even when one of your feet is off the cliff, and you're standing on just one foot. I faced such a situation three years ago.'

Raghav looks at Jayanti. Jayanti averts his gaze and starts tapping her pen on the desk, looking away. She seems embarrassed.

'My name is Raghav, and I am a character in a story. We are all characters in some way or the other. And we have to tell our story. Even a four-year-old knows how to speak, and that's all writing really is—speaking on a page.

'You can write into the air; you can speak on a page. A painting can be a novel, and a story can paint the perfect picture. Dance can express such emotion, and emotions can stir deep movements within even a chance observer. That's what a writer is. To become an authentic writer, sit in a chariot behind the twin horses of logic and emotion, and hold on tight for the ride of a lifetime. We are all storytellers, and all of us play different roles in our lives, isn't it? All of us have conflicts in our lives, but the resolution may vary from person to person. Every story can have multiple endings, just try to make it a remarkable one.'

'What are your conflicts?' someone from the crowd shouts.

Raghav grins, 'That'll be for some other session. We have other things planned for today.'

Raghav takes another hour to share his knowledge about the process of writing and how to start a story. Everyone in the auditorium just goes with the flow and asks many interesting questions. Only one person looks a little worried and not fully present—Jayanti. She has neither asked any question nor said anything during the workshop.

At the end of the workshop, she is waiting for the last person to exit the classroom when she approaches Raghav.

'Hi,' says Jayanti, coming up to the dais.

'Hi,' Raghav casually responds, closing the lid of his laptop and then switching off the projector. He continues gathering his things and putting them in his bag. He realizes that he was too harsh to her.

'It was a great session,' Jayanti says.

'Thank you,' Raghav smiles and accepts her praise gently.

'So, the example you shared with us, was it especially for this class or do you usually share that with everyone?' she asks.

'That's normal, I didn't have anything better to share at that moment,' Raghav responds with some hesitation and says, 'Never mind.'

After an awkward moment of silence, Raghav's cellphone goes off—it's an alarm.

'Excuse me, I am getting a call,' Raghav lies. Jayanti waits by the stairs hesitantly for a second and then walks out slowly towards the exit.

Raghav keeps the phone in his pocket.

∞

In a few minutes, Raghav, with his bag hanging on his left shoulder, heads towards the other exit of the auditorium. The cold breeze hits him, and he feels like he is standing in front of an iceberg, after having spent two years in Mumbai.

He walks towards the guest house, stopping by the lake just as the sun is about to touch the horizon. Sitting on the secluded bench near the sidewalk, he observes everything around him. The sunset is a smooth collusion of reds and yellows reflecting on the lake. Little birds are chirping on their way back home, their wings skimming the water over the lake. The moisture and cold in the air chills Raghav as he hugs himself and relives his memories.

'Are you feeling cold?'

Surprised, Raghav turns to find Jayanti standing behind him, just a few feet away. Her black eyes are glistening in the sunset. She looks incredibly beautiful as a light gust of wind lets loose strands of hair across her cheeks. He notices her earrings; they are the fish-shaped ones that he gifted her a long time ago.

Recovering from his daze, he gives her a fake smile. 'That's the weather here in January, isn't it?' he says.

'You didn't carry anything woolen?' she asks, noticing him shiver.

'I think I forgot to carry my earmuffs. It's okay, I am fine.'

Raghav rubs his hands to warm them and then rubs his cheeks and ears.

How time changes things—two people who have seen each other naked emotionally and literally now need to mask their emotions from each other. She steps closer. They are now standing next to each other, looking at the sunset.

'Even I don't have a jacket to give you like in a Bollywood movie,' Jayanti says jokingly.

'I don't need one, it's fine. So, how's Kavya?'

'She is fine. She is at home.'

'Yeah, I know. I messaged her before coming here.'

'She is returning today.'

'Tomorrow,' he said.

'Umm, yeah, tomorrow,' Jayanti responds hesitantly.

'You have changed over these three years,' Jayanti says. After a pause, she continues, 'When I feel low, I usually come here. This place makes me feel calm.'

'You know, you and I were born innocent, so if you or I feel that we have changed or become rebellious, it's absolutely a return gift to each other. And do you even feel low?' Raghav looks into her eyes.

These were words that Raghav should have said long back but never did in fear of losing her. Maybe he feels more free now. She looks embarrassed and does not have an answer to his question. There is a moment of silence between the two.

Sometimes silence is louder than words.

'I am sorry,' Jayanti says.

'I think "sorry" should have an expiry date. Well, it's been more than three years, you don't have to be sorry or feel sorry for anything now,' Raghav replies, with no hesitation or doubt. He continues, 'I spoke to my sister about you, and she told me, "Every now and then, a person with no agenda, no ulterior motive and no self-interest will take pleasure in helping you succeed, grow and live your purpose. This person will operate with love, will seek no praise and will want nothing in return. This person is a gift. Hold on to them." And do you remember what you said at the gate after my farewell? You said, "Never regret the things that happened." Now see the irony, I am sharing my regrets with the same person who said this to me. Nothing could be more painful than this. Do you even *feel* sorry?'

'Still, I wanted to say sorry,' Jayanti replies.

'I think I forgave you long back,' Raghav says, taking a step back.

'I think I should leave. It's getting colder,' she says.

'Sure.'

Raghav turns to leave, while Jayanti pauses for a moment. She then slowly heads to the other side of the lake.

∞

When Raghav has almost fallen asleep, someone knocks at his door. He jerks awake and checks the wall clock. It says 11.00 p.m. He wears his slippers, pulls the blanket around him and walks towards the door. Standing at the door is a man completely covered from top to bottom. He is wearing a monkey cap and has a stick in his hand. He looks scary in this attire.

'Sir, this is for you,' the man says and tries to give him a packet.

'Who are you?' a scared Raghav asks him. He holds the door tightly in case he needs to shut it on his face.

'Sir, I am the guard on duty today. I know you,' the man says.

'Aaah! You should have told me. Otherwise I would have kicked you in the balls right away,' Raghav says, sighing in relief.

'Why, sir?' he asks.

'Because you scared me. What's that?' Raghav asks, taking the package from him.

'Jayanti ma'am asked me to check if you are awake and then give it to you,' the guard says.

'Okay. Thank you,' Raghav says.

The man turns and heads away. Raghav watches him walk away.

He closes the door and inspects the packet curiously, wondering what could be in it. He opens the packet—it's a pair of blue earmuffs and a note that says, 'It will save you from shivering.'

Raghav wears the earmuff before he wraps himself in the blanket. He is finally warm and can sleep peacefully.

six

Raghav's narration of the events of the last four days is interrupted. The DCP has called all the officers to the meeting room.

'What happened?' asks Raghav.

'Don't go anywhere. I'll be back in some time,' says Naveen and tells the clerk to bring tea for Raghav.'

When they are all in the DCP's office, DCP Harsh Vardhan says, 'Delhi Police yesterday, acting on a tip-off, arrested seven people supplying counterfeit pharmaceuticals and arms in NCR. Delhi Police helped Sambhal Police, where they busted seven illegal arms factories in the last seven days by campaigning against the criminals making illicit weapons. This is usual, but what bothers us now and has kept us on tenterhooks is that these criminals have been identified as associated with gangsters in Uttar Pradesh. I got a call from the ministry, and we have been asked to control it. Officers, keep an eye on every case. Don't take anything lightly. The weakest link might connect the incidents and give the most substantial lead. Got it?'

'Yes, sir.'

'Naveen, What's the progress on the college case? Before it catches fire and the media turn at us, make sure we have something in hand to show.'

'Sure, sir. Awasthi and I are investigating the case, and I'll share an update with you soon.'

The walkie-talkie beeps. Awasthi steps back to respond.

'Hmm…okay,' the DCP nods and allows everyone to return to work.

'Sir, there is a situation in the IEC college,' says Awasthi, looking towards Naveen.

'What happened?' he asks.

'Sir, some of the students in support of college professor Ansari are raising slogans against the government and Uttar Pradesh Police, demanding justice for Ajay.'

'I know Ansari, and he is a professor in the chemistry department. We exchanged some words at the college,' adds Raghav.

'Awasthi! We need to leave for the college before it spreads further.'

'Sure, sir.' Awasthi follows him to his desk.

'Raghav, you come with me in the van. I'll drop you while coming back. This way, you'll also be able to gather some interesting facts about our work for your next book,' Awasthi winks.

'C'mon, let's get going,' says Naveen.

As the police vehicle hits the highway, with Awasthi at the wheels, Naveen turns towards Raghav and resumes questioning him, 'So, what happened after that?'

seven

8 January 2022. 11.00 a.m.

Today, there are more attendees than yesterday. Raghav can exactly match the faces with the seats. However, his eyes can't find Jayanti. He tries to find her in the auditorium with a cursory glance and begins, 'So, today, I am going to share the most crucial part that you must do before you begin to write your story. Remember, stories teach us to love, to forgive others and to strive to do better than we have done. Hence, you need to ask yourself—where are you in the story? The best story, the most excellent movie or the most exceptional documentary is created when it is inspired by real life.'

Raghav explains each detail of storytelling and story writing, and then he assigns everyone the task of writing a short story based on what they feel and what they want to write about. He then takes a round of the auditorium, while everyone is writing, and notices Jayanti in the extreme corner. He watches her in the crowded class; she is busy writing and hasn't seen him yet, so he gazes on. Raghav remembers how the first time he looked at Jayanti, it was as if every ounce of breath was taken from his lungs and he was floating in the air like midnight smoke. Every time she kissed him, it felt like the world stopped and everyone vanished, leaving just the two of them to wander the earth together. Every time she held his face between her hands, it felt like she was untying all of his knots. Then he remembers—just a few memories, not many—how she left him alone, helplessly crying and pleading with her to stay with him when he needed her the most. He discards the thought of thanking her for the care she showed yesterday by sending him the earmuffs.

Just like yesterday, Raghav is the last one to leave the auditorium. He takes the same route he took yesterday past the lake to reach the guest house. He spots Jayanti sitting on the secluded bench under a palash tree. He keeps walking, not stopping when he crosses the bench. As he passes by her, he feels like there is an eclipse—everything around him seems to vanish, and the sunset reflects blood red into the lake. There is dead silence. He feels cold, out of place. Jayanti does not speak a word. She just sits quietly, numb, waiting for him to say hi, at least. Raghav slowly disappears in the distance.

∞

It's 8.00 p.m., and Jayanti is now standing in front of Raghav's guest house, adjacent to the faculty apartments. She has greeted various faculty members 'good evening' seven times in the last 35 minutes. She feels a soft panic inside her, one that can grow or fade, depending on what she does next. It will fade if she backs away, but then she will have to do this again another time.

After some time, she sees Raghav coming out of his

room and walking towards the garden in front of the faculty accommodation.

'Hi, are you waiting for someone here?' Raghav asks, surprised at seeing her suddenly in front of the guest house. He looks around, and though another question arises in his mind, he doesn't ask.

'No, I was just passing by…' says Jayanti hesitantly.

She turns and walks away towards the hostels. Raghav doesn't know that she was waiting there for him. At times, people fail to understand the beauty of affection. Not everyone can feel it; not everyone can understand it either.

'Listen,' Raghav calls out before he changes his mind.

Jayanti turns around and pauses.

'Thank you for the earmuffs,' he says.

'No problem,' she replies and hesitates, as if she wants to say something.

'What happened?'

'I wanted to talk to you.'

'Yes, tell me?' Raghav says uncertainly and walks a few steps closer to her.

'I am sorry,' she says, her voice low, regretful. 'I know, you don't want to talk to me anymore, but I wanted to talk to you once.'

Her words are heavy and pleading. Jayanti used to be the one who neither felt nor said sorry for anything. Well, most of the time, she was right. She was right that their relationship was going to end one day.

'About what?' Raghav asks.

'You asked yesterday if I ever felt low in the last three years? And the answer is, yes, a lot. I feel low even today. Maybe I deserve this. I know that I should have said sorry to you.' Her face crumples sadly. 'I am sorry, Raghav, for the things I did to you and for the things I couldn't do.'

Raghav and Jayanti are looking into each other's eyes. A conversation that should have happened three years earlier, when it was most needed, is happening now.

Raghav then says, 'We were so immature in college, but after being on medication for nine months for depression and suicidal fear, I realized that sometimes in life, you should let go of things. Now I believe that if things don't happen according to what you expect, it means that it is not right for you. You know, when your life has been built on shifting sands, it is wise to seek a new life upon the rock...Well, that's all in the past now. It was tough for me too.'

'You could have at least stopped me,' Jayanti says defiantly.

'The first thing I did was to come and meet you. Do you know why? Because I needed you at that time. You said I was being overpossessive of you. When we are madly in love, it does not mean we are being possessive, it simply means that that person means a lot in our life. It's rare these days. If a relationship is strengthened bit by bit, then bit by bit, it can be broken too.' Raghav is finally opening up about these things that he has been suppressing for years.

Jayanti waits silently, wanting him to share more. She aches to know what he has been thinking, to know the feelings that were left without closure. 'Sorry.' Jayanti says again, sounding defeated, helpless and numb.

'That's okay. Anyway, there is no point in discussing the past,' Raghav nods and takes a few steps towards the sports ground. A vast blanket of white fog hangs heavy over the ground.

The freezing fog has wrapped up everything. He feels the same within. Jayanti follows him.

'Yeah. That's your favorite spot,' she says, pointing towards the bench in the ground where Raghav used to sit and talk to his parents for hours on the phone.

He smiles. 'Oh, yeah. So, how's your father now? Does he still get chocolates for you at CSD rates?' Raghav remembers the days when she used to get chocolates for all her friends whenever her father used to come to visit her. After Jayanti lost her mother to cancer a few months ago, her father took care of her, and would spoil her in every way possible.

'Papa is no more,' Jayanti says quietly, sitting down on the bench.

'What?' Raghav is shocked. He wants to tell her that things will be fine, but the right words refuse to come out. 'What happened to him?' is all he can manage. Despite the cold of the winter evening, he can feel his loose shirt start to cling to his back in places.

'I don't know,' Jayanti wipes her tears and presses her lips together.

'Meaning?' Raghav asks again. But he hesitates—she may not be comfortable sharing this. Asking about someone's death when he is a part of Indian Army is always painful.

'He was murdered.'

'Murdered? How? He was in the army. What happened? Are you okay talking about it?'

She nods.

One year ago. Mawai Village.

Jayanti wraps up her notebooks from the big wooden bench under the neem tree and gets ready to take a walk with her father around the farm. Her cousin Prashant is also with her. Her father reached home last night after eight months for a visit, and she is excited, waiting for him to get up and share stories of bravery with her.

'Good morning, beta! How are your studies going?' With his neatly groomed hair and tidy moustache, Jayanti's father Prakash looks proper and formal even at home. He walks up to Jayanti and pats her on the head.

Jayanti feels wildly happy with him here. 'Good morning, Papa. Studies are fine. Please have a seat.' She gets up from the bench and waits for her father to sit.

'Pranam, Chacha ji!' says Prashant, touching his feet.

'How are you, Prashant beta? How's your journalism going?' asks Prakash motioning him to sit.

'I am fine, Chacha ji! Have completed my exams; just waiting for results. I am trying to join as an intern at a news channel. Let's see,' says Prashant.

'Good, good! God bless you.'

'You both carry on, I'll come later,' Prashant says and leaves.

'You were sleeping when I reached last night,' Prakash tells Jayanti.

'Yes, I was waiting for you, and then I fell asleep. How are you?' Jayanti asks.

'Sit! I am good. Your aunt told me that you passed the exam with 9.6 CGPA. I am glad. Now you have to decide which way you will proceed—MBA or still want to crack SSB and join the army?'

Jayanti nods. 'Yes, Papa. I want to go for SSB, but I want your advice. However, I am not sure about this score. My last year of engineering is there, so I'll try to get as much as I can so that it helps when I join the army.'

'When you have this much, you don't need my advice. Actually no one needs any advice before joining the army. It's a matter of pride.'

'I want to be like you.'

Her father laughs, 'Why like me? You are better than I am. Just be the best version of yourself. Finish your studies and focus on your goal. If you work hard, you can make progress even after joining the army.'

'I know, Papa, but how many years will it take me to become a lieutenant general in the army?'

Her father sighs. 'It's not that easy, though not difficult too. You are just 22, a young girl. If you want to go for reattempt, go for it.'

'Yes, papa. You were also 18 when you joined the police.'

'I had no option to reattempt. I never wanted to join the police. I always wanted to join the army at a higher rank. I was good in studies like you, Jayanti, but your grandfather gave me only six months, and I failed. You do not have to worry about that, you take your time, and never give up.'

'Are you coming to the farm?' he asks after a pause.

'Yes, Papa. I've been waiting for you only.' Jayanti loves to talk to him. And this has increased even more from the time she started consciously trying to know him as a father and a soldier. The long conversations have made her a better daughter and a better human. Her father has been the initial fuel to her dream of joining the Indian Army.

In a moment, dark clouds rise from the horizon and cover the sky.

'I think it's going to rain soon. We can go some other time.'

'Papa, at what time you are leaving for Lucknow tomorrow?' Jayanti asks.

'Oh, I forgot, I have to leave today evening. I will take you along next time. There is something important I need to finish on the way,' Prakash says.

As they are talking, they hear the thrum of an engine. Prakash's friend is approaching him on a black Bullet. Prakash waves at him.

'Hey, Ansari, how are you?'

'Hey,' Ansari stops the bike under the neem tree.

'I am good. Good to see you, Prakash.' He takes off his sunglasses and places them in his shirt pocket. He wipes his face with a long handkerchief.

Ansari and Prakash are old friends, having grown up in the same area. While Prakash joined the police and then moved to the army, Ansari became a respected professor at IEC.

Ansari smiles at Jayanti.

'Pranam, uncle.'

'*Khush raho, beta*. How are you?'

'I am good.'

'Jayanti! Get something for uncle,' Prakash says.

Jayanti goes inside.

'So, how's duty going, Prakash? This time you came after so many months,' Ansari asks, sitting comfortably on the bike.

'Yeah, after eight months. I was not getting leave, but this time, I have come for a month,' Prakash tells him.

'That's good news.'

'You got this new beauty, Ansari,' Prakash pats the bike.

He nods, 'Last month. Come! We will go for a ride.'

'Let's have some tea first.'

'No, I am good. I will not have anything; come, we will be back in some time,' Ansari insists.

'Okay, let me grab my phone,' Prakash picks up his shirt from the wooden bench.

'We are just going nearby, why do you need a cellphone? Come.' Ansari starts the bike and shifts to the back seat, letting Prakash ride.

Jayanti returns with the tea, only to find her father leaving.

'I will come back in some time, Jayanti,' Prakash says and accelerates the bike.

Three kilometres away from Dullapur, where they pass by a paan shop at the T-junction, Ansari asks Prakash to stop, 'Let's have paan.'

Ansari's cellphone rings. Ansari picks up the call and talks for a minute. 'Prakash, I need to go,' he says. He keeps the phone in his pocket, chewing his paan.

'What happened? Is everything fine?' Prakash asks, concerned.

'Yes. Take the bike home. I'll reach more quickly this way,' Ansari points at the path through the fields that will take him to his house.

'Take this. I'll take a walk through the fields. It has been months…' smiles Prakash and gives him the keys.

'Are you sure?' asks Ansari.

'Yes, and come home in the afternoon. Let's talk over lunch.'

Ansari heads off straight, while Prakash takes a left through the fields. On one side of the path, there are huge corn stalks, a common sight in winter season, while on the other side, there are paddy fields as far as the eye can see.

Suddenly, Prakash notices someone following him. He quickens his steps down a narrow pathway between two cornfields.

He sees three people approaching him with pistols in their hands, ready to attack any minute. He starts running. A bullet grazes the side of his head. He searches for his cellphone in his pocket, but it is not there.

He takes the shortest path to the other side of the canal at the edge of the cornfields. The men chase him through the cornfield.

Prakash sees a big sugarcane farm, and then in a split second, he feels the cold chill and air gusts in his throat. He does not stop and rushes forward, shouting. Gunshots, one after the other. More shouting. More screaming. More running. The attack is fierce, efficient and deadly.

He cannot breathe. It feels as if someone is choking him. His heart is racing, and all he wants to do is curl up into a ball and wait for someone to save his life. But no one will; no one is there. A choked cry for help forces itself up his throat, and he feels a drop run down his cheek when another bullet hits his shoulder. This seems to be the end of the road for him. His head jerks back, and he falls on the side of the canal.

The men approach and raise their guns. He can barely make out the trees through the misty veil surrounding his eyes. They look like bony fingers stretching for the dark sunless sky.

Shots are fired. He can feel his heart beating against his rib cage, slowing every second. Realization dawns on him—he is going to die. He tries to suck in air, but none comes.

Tears fall down his cheeks, and he can taste blood in his mouth.

He sees a tall shadow in front of him. Before he turns, a rod strikes his skull.

As the life drains out of him, his stomach feels sick. One by one, he loses control of his limbs until finally his head slumps to the ground. His mind gives one final sigh. Then he feels nothing, nothing at all. There's only darkness as he slips into death.

∞

Profuse tears start rolling down Jayanti's face as she finishes narrating the story. She remembers clearly how the body was found and the deadening sadness she's felt since that day, that nothing seems to help.

'The FIR was registered under A74 CrPC and the charge sheet was submitted by the police, but soon after, the case was closed. I tried to file an appeal, but my uncles told me to concentrate on my studies and complete my college degree because court cases in India never end, and I need to look after myself even while looking for justice for my father. However, for the last one year, I couldn't get a night of proper sleep. His friend Ansari Chacha, the professor from the chemistry department, helped me to get a hostel room in the college, but whenever I ask him about my father and what happened that day, because he was the last person who was with him, he avoids the conversation. I even asked him if he could help me to file an appeal in the high court to reopen the case, and he's been avoiding talking to me after that. He said that he has sympathy for me, but he can't go beyond that.'

Jayanti adds, 'Will you help me? I want to file appeal in the high court to reopen the case. I know I can't do it alone. I could only stop myself because I had to complete my degree. Now it is about to be complete. Will you help me?'

Jayanti knows how important it is to get a job so that she can pay all the loans and then look ahead in her career. Since her father's death, her wish to join the army has waned. She has lost some of that idealism and become more practical. However, she does not want to compromise on the investigation into her father's death, and she is trying day in and day out to find a clue that will help her solve it.

Raghav observes her briefly. He then asks, 'So, is it true that you invited me here for the workshop? Was this the only reason to call me? You could have asked me over a call. I would have helped as much as I could.'

Jayanti nods in affirmation, 'I didn't know if you would ever meet me again. I wanted to meet you once, and this was the one possible way I could. I hope you are not taking me in the wrong way. I always loved you and that is the reason I am sharing this with you. We may have different points of view, but that does not make two people wrong in anyway.'

'You haven't forgotten me?' Raghav has been wanting to know the answer to that for a long time.

'How could I forget those days? Could you forget me?'

The two have known each other for years, but after listening to Jayanti, Raghav wants to help her as much as he can. But he is unsure about how to react to the situation, which is not easy at all.

Jayanti can see frozen snot forming around his nose. Raghav tries to control his chattering teeth. The weather seems to be trying its best to get them to hold hands and keep them warm, just like they used to do years before. Jayanti smiles, looking at him.

'What?' asks Raghav through rattling teeth.

'Nothing, you have changed. You are not suited to this weather anymore,' Jayanti rubs her hands to generate some warmth.

'I forgot to carry your earmuffs,' Raghav says and puts his hands in his jacket pockets.

'Those you can wear at night. I think it's a better idea for you to go back to your room and take rest. You've had a long day,' she says and offers him a candy to munch on. It's his favourite.

'Yeah, I think so...thanks,' Raghav sets off and then turns back. 'Tomorrow we are wrapping up early. We can go to the cafeteria after lunch, if you are free?'

'Yeah, sure,' she says. There is velvet softness in her voice.

Raghav nods and they go their own ways.

They both know that the magical thing about love is that it is equally mystic, whether it happened years earlier or it is happening now. They just need to take this ahead—towards each other, not away.

eight

9 January 2022. 3.00 p.m.

Raghav walks into the cafeteria and spots Jayanti sitting in the corner, writing something in a notebook.

The cafeteria is a sort of vast coffee shop in the evening, yet one can stay all day and feel good even if one buys nothing at all. That's what makes it special. It is a place that welcomes everyone, rather than treating the students as 'customers'. This is not a money-nexus venue but a memories-nexus space, and that makes it a real gem in this college. Jayanti looks adorable in a navy-blue blazer. She looks so different in college uniform. Raghav can't imagine how he used to look in college uniform when he was in the first year of college—skinny and shapeless. Yes, he describes himself with these two words.

'Hi,' Raghav says, standing next to her while she is solving some questions.

'Hey, hi! Please sit,' Jayanti shifts her books aside and drags a chair for him.

Raghav sits on the chair and notices some of the doodles in her notebook. 'So, doodling is still your favorite hobby. Haven't you thought about pursuing it?' Raghav points at the notebook before she closes it.

She looks confused, then laughs. 'Oh, never you mind! I doodled these during some lectures. That's it.'

'So, how's placement going?' Raghav starts the conversation with the most crucial question.

'Companies are supposed to visit from next month. I hope I get selected. By the way, why did you leave your job?' Jayanti asks.

'I worked for two years. I think that was enough for me. I feel content now,' Raghav says, flipping through her notebook.

'Yes, yes, you should be. So, does this canteen look the same as it used to be when you were in first year?' she asks. Her face is thoughtful, as if she has something on her mind.

'Not at all. But yeah, it was fun. There is a place behind the cafeteria; it wasn't allowed then, but we used to go there for a walk after dinner,' Raghav points to the area behind the cafeteria.

'Even now it's not allowed. We only know that it used to be called lovers' point...right?' Jayanti says.

Raghav laughs out loud, 'Why, you want to go there? Yeah…'

'I haven't been there in all this time. It's not allowed, but Kavya knows about it. I think she's been there once,' she said.

Kavya is Jayanti's roommate now. She was the one who introduced Raghav and Jayanti. In fact, she was the messenger between them in the early days of their romance.

'I wanted to tell you that after this workshop, I am going to meet my cousin Naveen, who is an IPS officer currently posted in Lucknow…'

Jayanti nods, 'Really?'

'If you want, you can come with me and tell him the whole thing. I am sure he will help you,' Raghav informs her.

'Thank you so much, Raghav!'

'No problem. You want anything, coffee or tea?' asks Raghav.

'I'll have coffee.'

'I'll get one for you.'

Raghav gets up to get coffee from the counter while Jayanti shifts to a bigger table, keeping her things in her bag. Jayanti pulls a chair for him to sit next to her. Raghav keeps the cups on the table and settles down.

'Let's go there?' Jayanti points towards the back side of the cafeteria through the windows.

'Are you sure? What if someone sees us?' Raghav asks while stirring his coffee.

'Yes, but you are a guest. If someone catches us, I'll say that you wanted to visit the place. You wanted to see the entire college,' says Jayanti, her face serious.

'No way!'

'I am joking.'

'I know you. Okay, let's go...' Raghav leaves the half-filled coffee cup on the table. They exit the cafeteria and stroll through the lane between the hostels. The sun has touched the horizon.

After walking some more, they pause at a cluster of small trees. Golden light is piercing through the the leaves, and ahead of them, the fountain is making a soft sound of falling water.

'Jayanti.'

'Yes, Raghav.'

'I wanted to ask you yesterday itself. Who is this Guruji? Seems like the marketing team has done a great work getting big sponsors from the city.'

'Oh, he is our chief guest. Guruji is visiting our college with Chief Minister Shiv Narayan.' Jayanti him tells about the recent achievements of the college under the schemes of the Uttar Pradesh government.

'I saw some banners across the academic block,' Raghav observes.

'He is very, very respected in Ayodhya. Especially after all the contribution he made towards leading all sadhus and sants for the work on the temple and in encouraging people to contribute funds for the temple. He also has a great ashram in Ayodhya.'

'Looks like. Must be a good leader too,' Raghav nods.

'What happened? What are you thinking?' asks Jayanti.

'Nothing,' Raghav replies, enjoying these quiet moments with Jayanti.

The air is cold. There is no one around at this hour. The place does not have a good vibe at all.

'It reminds me of a place where hyenas live,' says Raghav.

'I'm sorry about this. I didn't know it would be like this.'

'That's okay.'

'They must have cleared the space for preparations,' says Jayanti pointing towards the men assembling bamboo poles at the very end of the area. 'It used to be a beautiful place. Now it looks barren, doesn't it?' On reaching the fountain, Raghav sits under the shadow of a tree.

'So, did you meet anyone in the last three years?'

'I met many people at college, but everyone seemed more interested in my size than my wishes,' shares Jayanti. There is disappointment in her voice. 'What about you? Did you forget me in these three years?' Now it is her turn.

'No. I thought you were the most perfect girl I ever met.

I would stay up every night, waiting for the chance to see you again the next day. I thought about the many anniversaries we would have: the presents, the smiles. I wanted you more than anything.'

Jayanti remains silent.

'But you never gave me that chance. We don't always get what we wish for. Was I emotionally weak? Is that what bothered you so much that you left me? Now you can tell the truth,' Raghav says with a grin.

'After losing you, I realized what happened. It started with being with you, sharing everything with you. But then, over a period, I started asking for space. But this affects you the most when that person is not around. I was a kid,' Jayanti confesses.

'And now? You think you have grown up?'

'I think so...' Jayanti says.

Raghav's phone beeps. It's a reminder that he has set to work on the draft of his new book. The moment is lost. He snoozes it and asks, 'Do you know at what time tomorrow the driver will arrive for pick-up?'

'You can ask the dean to extend your stay if you want to spend one more day on campus,' she suggests.

'I wish I could, and I want to, but I need to leave,' says Raghav. An emotional turmoil is being witnessed by both—he does not know when he will meet her again, and she doesn't want him to leave.

She nods, 'I'll check with logistics and message you. When are you planning to meet Naveen?'

'I'll meet him on the way,' Raghav answers and offers her his cellphone to enter her number.

Jayanti responds and smiles, 'I have your number.'

Raghav knows this moment and feeling calls for a kiss but suppresses the urge.

There's a sudden breeze, and it carries a sharp chemical stench. It's something that usually comes from the chemistry department. Both press their hands to their nose.

'Let's go. Coming here was a bad idea.' Jayanti turns and they walk back down the same lane between the hostels through which they came.

'Wait.'

'What happened?' Jayanti asks.

'Can you come with me?'

She nods, and they turn down the same path again, 'You forgot something?'

'Yes, something important,' Raghav stops her, looks around, and comes closer.

'What are you doing?' she asks nervously.

In this short period between thoughts and conversation, he feels he must kiss her right now without thinking. In that kiss would be the sweetness of enthusiasm, a million warm thoughts condensed into a moment.

'Found,' he says, looking into her eyes.

'What?'

'Something vital I had forgotten.'

She bursts out laughing.

'I must tell you, you don't overuse your brain. You spend it correctly, precisely,' she gives a sensuous smile and adds, 'Let's go now. And thank you once again for the help.'

'You owe me a kiss then.'

'I do. You will be paid in full when we meet tonight.'

The sun sinks lower in the sky, the light of day draining

away, giving way to the velvety dark of the winter evening—colours subdued in the fading light accompanied by a cold breeze. Love is what makes us who we are, and it is the energy that brings us to life. That's what love can do: fix souls, fix the mind, cure us all.

nine

9 January 2022. 9.00 p.m.

Raghav is walking quickly towards the playground surrounded by small trees on all sides. He takes a sharp turn towards the guest house. He suddenly gets goosebumps, sensing that someone is following him. It's eerily dark, and the feeling gets stronger. The last vehicle passed at least 10–12 minutes ago. There are no lights on, and he can see the light from the windows in the boys' hostel some distance away. His skin tingles, he breathes deeper and tries to listen with greater intensity. His vision becomes sharper. Then, slowly, he turns, expecting to find a dog, a bird or just the guard. But there's nothing there. He walks faster towards his room, breaking into a sprint the last few meters. He locks the door as soon as he enters.

Raghav sits on the chair and tries to breathe. He can feel his heartbeat like a clock ticking. He pours some water for himself and calls Jayanti, but her phone keeps ringing. Jayanti does not respond.

A few minutes later, Raghav hears someone knocking at the door. He picks up his cellphone, not opening the door yet. He feels the acute need for a door with a peephole.

There are a few knocks again at the door. Raghav searches Naveen's number and keeps it on speed dial.

He walks towards and door and pulls it open. Professor Ansari is standing at his doorstep. He is wearing a white kurta, *taqiyah* on his head. A muffler is wrapped round his neck twice.

'Hello, sir,' Raghav says, surprised. 'What brings you are here at this hour?' Raghav is reminded of the conversation he had with him earlier.

'Hello, may I come in?' Professor Ansari asks him.

'Sure, please come,' Raghav lets him in and drops his phone on the bed. He offers the professor a chair.

'You please sit,' says the professor.

Raghav settles on the corner of the bed in front of him.

'I wanted to talk to you about something important, so I thought I'll come here and personally meet you,' Professor Ansari says, sitting down and loosening one fold of his muffler.

'Yes, please tell me,' replies Raghav. Raghav suspects that either the professor wants to make him understand the equality between these two religions or he has an opinion about his community.

'I am not sure how much money you make from your writing or workshops,' Professor Ansari begins. 'But I wanted to make you an offer. If you work with me and my friends, we can help each other grow. We are a group of various people, from media houses to universities. We can support you in all ways, from your books to your speeches, and your publicity. They all will take care of your social image as well. They will also help you financially.'

'Wait, you want me to work with you? What kind of work

are you talking about?' Raghav is surprised at this sudden offer, but it interests him.

'I mean, I told you earlier as well that people listen to you. So, we want you speak about us in gatherings or if you can write great stories about Islam.'

Raghav remains silent.

The professor adds, 'I am not asking you to change your religion. In our community, there are not many authors. The few who are there always speak against us. They don't have any knowledge about the purity of Islam and the peace we want.'

'Sir, thank you for your offer, but I am happy with what I am writing. What I am writing is good enough to do well in the market. You are offering me money and fame, but I don't think I can do it.' Raghav wants to reject the offer more bluntly, but he stops himself from being rude.

'*Bismillah Hir Rahman Nir Raheem*. You should give it a second thought.'

'My first thought is to reject the offer, so there is no point giving it a second thought. You are trying to bribe me to speak for you. I'm sure some people can do it, but at least an author like me will never do it.'

'Bribing? You are getting me wrong, Raghav! We are offering you a job that you should consider. It's for your good.'

'Sir, when I write, I write like a boss. So, I don't need your job. You can find someone else to write your propaganda for you. I respect you as a guru. I respect your religion as I do mine. However, what you are asking me to do is beyond my knowledge and conscience.'

'No! I am not doing that,' says Professor Ansari, now furious.

'Subconsciously, that's what you are asking me to do. You're talking about equality, but you're actually promoting one religion over another. I am sorry, but please leave now.'

There is no sound in the room. Raghav gets up and walks out of the room. The air is so brittle it could snap.

Professor Ansari remains silent and follows him out of the room. When he is about to cross him, Raghav turns and says, 'And, sir...' The professor turns and pauses. 'No one has taken the mosque from you. They have just taken back what belongs to them. That's the best part of this nation. No one can take anything from you, what belongs to you belongs to you. Good night.'

Hiding behind the adrenaline, Raghav can feel the fear in his chest waiting to take over.

∞

It's probably Jayanti at the door. Raghav opens the door.

'Hey, sorry, I missed your calls. I was just coming to meet you. Please come,' says Raghav, and Jayanti enters. Raghav closes the door and locks it.

'What happened? Are you okay? Thirteen calls back to back?'

'I went out for a walk half an hour ago. Someone was following me.'

'Who will follow you, Raghav? Must be the security guard. They wear muffler and cover the face, so you must have thought something shady is happening.'

'No, it was not the guard. It was someone else,' Raghav says, and a sharp chill runs down his spine.

'Okay, if you say so. I got this for you,' Jayanti gives him a packet of food. 'Also, I found out about your departure. Your cab will arrive at 4.00 p.m. so that you reach the airport on time.'

'Okay, thanks. You want coffee?' asks Raghav.

'Sure,' she says.

'By the way, why didn't you mention that the campus looks insanely beautiful from the terrace?' Raghav asks her. 'The fountain you mentioned near the other gate of the college is breathtaking in the moonlight.'

'Oh! Did you see it? We don't have access to the terrace of any of the hostels. But you have that privilege,' she grins.

Jayanti gets up from the chair and helps Raghav pour the coffee in two cups. The air in the room is thick with the scent of coffee.

'Take this, Let's go! I'll show you,' Raghav hands her a coffee mug.

'No. I am good. Maybe some other time.'

'C'mon, it's just the terrace,' Raghav insists.

'Are you sure? I don't know if it's allowed or not.'

'I went there yesterday, so I think we can go.'

'I mean. First of all, I am not even allowed to be here right now. Second, going there is taking too much risk for the thrill. We'll have to return quickly…'

In a few minutes, they reach the terrace. They are standing next to each other, looking at the lake from the top. A soothing but cold breeze is blowing from the water. Jayanti takes a sip of the coffee. A fleeting expression of rapture passes over her face. She is smiling broadly, enjoying the beauty of the scene. He glances down at the mug, thick, ceramic, cold to touch. They keep the cups on the ledge.

That welcome moonlight is a bit of pure luck, as the darkening sky is filled with lavender and indigo clouds, covering up the first stars of the night. Time seems to have slowed down for both of them. The yellow street light in front of them casts a warm glow on them, lighting their faces.

'It is so nice to be here,' says Jayanti. Raghav is deep in thought, and he doesn't reply.

'What are you thinking?' Jayanti breaks his reverie.

'Nothing. Just recalling our memories in this college. I don't know when we'll meet again,' Raghav says.

Jayanti reaches out to him, almost touching his hand, and says, 'Raghav, I wanted to say something.'

'Yeah…'

'Looking back, I sometimes think how I messed up things. I regret my actions completely. Is it too much to ask you to love me again even after three years? I want to get back together, and I know, this time, it will be more whole and alive than ever.' She moves closer to him. 'Can I come back?' she whispers hesitantly.

Raghav is just staring at her, listening to her. He wants to listen right now. Love is the sixth sense. Learn to listen, to feel, to sense it. That simple action transforms life. It did for them. Uncontainable happiness spreads on his face.

She hasn't moved a step closer from there—she is waiting for Raghav to respond.

Raghav takes the initiative. He steps closer to her. He breathes in her scent and takes her soft hand in his own.

'What happened?' she asks, gazing at him.

'Nothing, I like looking at you…I have always loved looking at you, whether you were around or not.' He comes closer and holds her by her shoulders. She looks so fragile at the moment. He feels that he is holding happiness and the satisfaction of all the time he missed in his life after going away from her. He confesses that romance is never cheesy. It's life. It's them. It's the moment under the sky right now, right here.

Jayanti breaks the silence, 'By the way, you always wanted to romance under the moon. Today, we have stars also, and that too in the guest house of Indian Engineering College! There can be nothing more thrilling than this.'

Raghav and Jayanti laugh, covering their face to avoid making any noise.

'Let's go,' says Jayanti, shivering in the cold breeze on her face.

Raghav runs his fingers up her arm, and then her cheeks. She almost closes her eyes to feel his touch. He then touches her lips, and her lips start quivering. She comes closer and can feel the warmth of his breath on her lips. He kisses her softly. Coffee wouldn't taste the same anymore.

Love takes its own route. No planning ever works in this sphere. Knowing this, Raghav holds her tightly in his arms. Neither of them want this moment to end. They hold on to each other, fearing that all this will vanish if they let go.

'I love you,' Jayanti says, looking into his eyes.

Everything runs like a montage in his mind. Once again, the thought occurs to him, this time, with certainty—love, the foundation of every problem and, sometimes, a solution too. He gazes at her.

'I love you too. Took you long enough to say it,' he replies, kissing her hands.

'I think I have been really stupid all these years, but it's better late than never.'

Whether it was a conscious effort or destiny that brought them together again, and in the very same college campus where they first met, is a question to which neither of them have the answer.

Suddenly, Raghav releases her. Someone is standing at the window of the faculty house and looking at them.

'I think someone saw us,' he says abruptly.

'What? Are you serious? Fuck!' Jayanti moves back, trying to hide, and pulls Raghav in the shadow of the wall.

'Shit!' The person has come out on the balcony now.

'I am so sorry for calling you here,' he says. He knows how it can affect her. Placement season is starting next month, and if there's some disciplinary action taken now, it's going to be a black mark on her CV.

'It's okay. I'll leave now, and I have not entered my name in the register. So, if someone asks you tomorrow, please tell them that I didn't meet you. Rest, I'll manage,' says Jayanti heading downstairs.

When they are downstairs, standing in front of the room, Raghav says, 'Okay, hope everything is fine, I don't want to be any kind of a problem for you.' He is waiting to see if Jayanti will come inside or leave.

'It's okay, no one has seen us,' she says and comes closer to him, almost half inside the door. She touches his cheeks, '…and I love you.'

This time Raghav pulls her inside.

'I should leave…' Jayanti doesn't complete her words, but her eyes convey that she definitely does not want to let go of this moment.

Raghav holds her hand.

She kisses him. Their eyes meet, and they are carried away to another world. She comes in and pushes him down on the bed and gets on top of him, running her hand over his chest, kissing him passionately.

'Are you being wild?' Raghav asks.

'Lock the door and be quiet,' Jayanti says as Raghav slowly caresses her neck.

He knows he is living a dream with his eyes open.

Raghav runs his hand through her hair. He has never felt this before. They have made love earlier, but they have been apart for so long that there are only flashes of intense passion and love between them.

'I have never done that before,' she says, looking at him once more. 'But first, check the curtains and turn off the lights.'

'Okay,' Raghav gets up to draw the curtains.

'Lights?'

'I want to see you,' Raghav dims the lights in the room. The room is a little darker now, but they can see each other clearly.

They hug each other and then Raghav pulls up her shirt a little bit. 'Take this off,' Raghav says in passionate anticipation.

Jayanti raises her arms, and he pulls her shirt off and throws it to the other side of the bed. He reaches down her thighs. With his every touch on her body, she feels euphoric and is not afraid to show it. Just when Raghav slides his hand down her belly, she clutches his hand tightly.

'Raghav…'

'Remove this,' Raghav pulls down her pants as she opens the buttons and unzips it. She looks conscious and nervous for a moment, but Raghav does not let the spark go away with his kisses and his caresses.

Jayanti removes his shirt. Unable to control her excitement, she sits on him and starts kissing his chest. It seems she has taken the reins, and Raghav is just mesmerized and spellbound watching this new side of her.

But he can't help himself and grabs her. He feels the softness of her body, and she closes her eyes. Raghav pushes her back on the bed and kisses her softly.

Jayanti takes off her bra, and she goes down on him.

It's time for Raghav to turn her around. This time he goes down on her, kissing every inch of her body. He can literally taste the sweetness of this moment. Jayanti feels a current passing through her body. He can feel her respond to every touch of his. Her toes are tingly. He takes control and starts stroking till she moans. She locks him between her legs. She is tender and covered in sweat. Suddenly, his muscles relax, and then he feels too sensitive to be touched anymore.

'Jayanti, you have to promise me that if there is anything bothering you, you have to share with me,' he tells her as he leans forward to hug her.

'Who else, of course...but what made you to say so all of a sudden,' she smiles.

'Just felt like saying this,' Raghav runs his hand from her shoulder to her hands.

No one needs a castle in the desert, just a warm hug and hope from the person you admire the most. Raghav pampers and consoles her. That's the power of emotional support.

'Now I should go,' Jayanti checks her cellphone and puts it on silent.

Raghav nods, 'Go and take rest. And just focus on your health from today.' He gives a quick kiss on her cheek before she opens the door and leaves.

Jayanti heads quietly to her hostel, hiding in the shadows.

Raghav goes into his room and closes the door. They are both unable to imagine the consequences of the situation.

Raghav convinces himself that this is not going to create any problem for the two of them. Even if there is anything, he needs to face it. He tells himself that he is going to make things right for the person he loves.

Jayanti reaches her hostel and drops Raghav a text that she has reached.

ten

10 January 2022. 7.00 a.m.

Raghav hears some low continuous knocks at the door. He opens the door, irritated. It is the same guard who handed over Jayanti's packet.

'Sir, are you leaving today?' he asks and peeps inside.

'Yes, I am, in some time. What happened?'

'I think your cellphone is off. Sudeep told me to inform you that Dean sir wants to meet you at 11.30 a.m. in his office,' the guard says.

Raghav nods, 'Okay. Thank you.' The guard leaves. A cold chill runs down his spine. He is not worried about himself but about Jayanti.

Raghav reaches the academic block. He leaves his luggage with the guard and waits in front of the dean's cabin. Dr Girish Dwivedi, the dean, approaches the cabin, and Raghav greets him.

'Call Jayanti also. You can come into the office after 10 minutes,' Dr Girish Dwivedi says, walking into his office. Raghav calls Jayanti and tells her to reach as soon as possible.

When she arrives, Raghav explains, 'The dean has called both of us to his office.'

'Don't worry, just tell him what we discussed, that we didn't meet yesterday.'

'He asked me to call you as well.'

'What?' Jayanti is now shocked. She adds, checking the time, 'I have my class in half an hour. But I will skip it. What happened to you? Why do you look so scared?'

Now, the two are standing and looking at the ticking of the giant clock hanging in the academic block.

'I am fine. Maybe just in a hurry to leave.'

After 10 minutes, Raghav knocks on the door and opens it just two inches and peeps in. 'May I come in, sir?' he asks.

Dean Girish Dwivedi beckons him in while he finishes signing a file and closes it.

Raghav and Jayanti enter. There is an L-shaped sofa on one side of the big office, and two black chairs are in front of his table. He points to a chair, indicating to Raghav that he should take a seat. Jayanti is standing next to the sofa. There are portraits of Mahatma Gandhi and Lal Bahadur Shastri on the wall just behind his chair. Professor Ansari is sitting and reading the newspaper at the other end of the sofa. His presence makes Raghav uncomfortable after the discussion they had yesterday. Fear is completely visible on his face, which he tries to hide.

'Do you know why you both are here?' the dean asks them. First, he looks at Jayanti and then his gaze shifts to Raghav.

'No, sir,' says Jayanti. At the same time, Raghav says, 'Yes, sir.'

Raghav and Jayanti look at each other, and in sync, both say, 'No, sir.'

The dean raises his eyebrows and turns to look at Raghav.

'You are an alum of this college. You should know and respect the policy of this place. Do you respect that?'

Raghav nods, 'Yes, sir.'

He continues, 'Do you know that we create walls between the hostels of juniors and seniors for the first three months after admission, and do you know why?

Jayanti and Raghav shake their heads.

'To avoid ragging and to mitigate the risk of anything that is not acceptable in this college. If you knew about it, then why did you both go to the restricted area?' asks the dean.

Both Raghav and Jayanti's faces are blank. Before they can say anything, the dean continues, 'The area behind the cafeteria is restricted. And you both were seen taking a walk in that area last evening. Is it true?'

'Yes sir,' Raghav accepts the accusation before he is asked about anything else. He takes a long breath.

'You are an ex-student of this college, you should know where to go and where not to go,' says Professor Ansari, folding the newspaper and keeping it in the newspaper basket.

'There are some rules. You both should know. What kind of impression are you leaving on your juniors?'

'My apologies, sir.' Jayanti steps forward.

'Sorry, sir. I didn't know. I asked Jayanti to take me around the college,' Raghav apologizes.

The dean gives him a paper, which seems like an apology letter, and asks both of them to sign it.

'You are an example for everyone here, don't be a wrong one,' he says, smiling at Raghav.

Raghav nods in agreement and says, 'Thank you, sir. Looking forward to coming here again.'

Raghav signs it after reading the first few lines quickly, and they take permission to leave.

While Jayanti is still inside the office, Professor Ansari takes Raghav out and whispers, 'Leave the college right now, else you will have to pay a price that you have never imagined. You have absolutely no idea who I am. I was just talking to you nicely until now, but you showed me your arrogance.' The professor glares at him.

'Sir, what are you talking about? You are unnecessarily trying to threaten me.'

'I am warning you. Just leave,' says Ansari and waves at some students far away.

Raghav prefers not saying anything and just leaves.

∞

Raghav is due to leave on the same day and tells Jayanti to meet Naveen before his departure.

He drags his trolley and bids farewell to other faculty members and students in the block. 'The cab has reached the gate,' Jayanti says. Jayanti and Raghav head towards the college gate.

'I had heard that time has wings, but you know, today I feel love also has wings. Thank you for letting me in your life once again,' Jayanti says with a happy smile on her face.

'You are welcome,' Raghav grins and keeps his bag on the back seat of the cab and sits in the passenger seat. He adds, 'Take care of yourself. I'll see you soon.'

'Yeah, I will. Thank you,' she responds. 'You need to make your entry in the register,' Jayanti tells the driver who steps out of the cab to do so.

In those brief moments, Jayanti presses her lips against his, and whispers in his ears, 'We need to build a library at our home.'

She is referring to his fantasy of making love in a library.

'For sure...' Raghav blushes.

Before the driver returns, Jayanti hands him a diary.

'This is for you. Have a safe flight, Raghav Sharma. I'll miss you.'

They both smile. The college gate opens. He remembers having thousands of mixed emotions while entering the gate four days back and now leaving with one emotion which rules all—love. Everyone's life is like a story, and we all live as characters of that story. It is up to us to strive for the perfect ending we wish for. Raghav and Jayanti wrote their names not just on the apology letter, but they also signed their names for a new beginning to their story.

Just then, a security guard shouts from the dean's office to the guard at the gate, 'Close the gate, no one will go out and no will enter without permission. It's an order. It's an order from the dean.'

Jayanti approaches the car, and Raghav comes out to find out what the matter is. They both go to the office to talk to the guard.

'Sir, it's an order from the dean. Someone has fallen from the hostel building, and the police are coming. You can't go out. You must take permission to leave. Please clear out the way and go back.'

'But who is it?' Jayanti asks, shocked.

'Ajay from fourth year. He was a bright student. He used to come in the night sometimes to have tea at the gate.'

Raghav and Jayanti run to the hostel. Breathless and sweaty,

Raghav runs towards the guard outside the hostel to ask what happened, with Jayanti following close behind.

All the corridors are packed with people, and everything is at a standstill before the siren of a police vehicle breaks the silence. As the police vehicle stops outside the hostel, Ajay is lying on the floor, still and bloody.

The police vehicle stops. Naveen and Awasthi clear the crowd and proceed to question the guard.

eleven

17 January 2022. 9.00 a.m.

Good morning and welcome! This is Ranjana Kapoor bringing you the most sensational news of the country.
   1,838 bottles of fake syrup of 450 ml each from a godown of another pharma firm based in Roorkee, Uttarakhand, have been seized. STF officials said the arrested accused was identified as a Lucknow resident named Vishal Agarwal, the owner of Hare Krishna Pharma. They said Agarwal manufactured this fake syrup with the brand name 'Dr Gaso' through the company named Liquid Formulation Pvt. Ltd and supplied it to different medical agencies in Lucknow and its adjoining districts, such as Gonda, Barabanki and Ayodhya, among many others.
   Deputy Superintendent of Police, STF, Vivek Kumar Singh, Uttarakhand, said that the STF initiated an investigation on the complaint of Harendra Singh of High Life Sciences Pvt. Ltd of Basti, the original manufactures and supplier of the Dr Gaso syrup. He said the counterfeit

syrup was manufactured cheaply and supplied in the market at retail price.

Medicines manufactured to save human lives have now become a cause of fear among people. The death rate in the country as well as in the state has increased significantly. Corruption, unemployment and crime have still not been eliminated from the nation even after 75 years. This the sorry state of governance in the country!

Who is responsible for these human lives? You can leave your vote on our Twitter handle.

This is not the end, my friends. In one of the prestigious colleges of UP, Indian Engineering College, Lucknow, which ranks in the top colleges of India, the death of fourth-year student Ajay Nagar remains unsolved one week after his body was found under suspicious circumstances in the college campus. The UP Police have been unable to declare for sure if the incident was a suicide or murder.

Awasthi mutes the volume of the TV and keeps the remote in his drawer.

'Naveen, what is the progress in the IEC suicide case?' asks the DCP while entering his cabin. He looks dead serious.

Naveen follows him and answers, 'Sir, I am on it.'

'And?'

'Sir, I just need to do some investigation. I am making progress on the case.'

'I need the charge sheet, Naveen, not your investigation procedure. You might be good at that, but I need results.'

'Yes, sir,' replies Naveen.

Naveen feels anxiety rise and flow from his fingertips. He

pulls open his drawer and takes out a strip of medicine—Atvian—with just four pills remaining out of 10. He gulps down the tablet with a glass of water.

'Sir, are you okay?' Awasthi asks, noticing him.

'I am fine,' Naveen snaps back and gets down to work. 'We need to go to the college tomorrow morning for regular investigation. Please inform the college about it. If they say classes are ongoing and will get disturbed, then tell them it's urgent. If they disagree, patch me over the call,' Naveen instructs. 'Also, Awasthi…' he adds.

'Yes, sir.'

'Can you find the closure report of the Prakash Shukla murder case? I want to go through it. Don't tell anyone about it.'

'Sir, why Prakash?'

'Awasthi, that Raghav's friend…Jayanti mentioned that Prakash and Ansari were friends. If Prakash lives in Barabanki and Ansari lives here, that means there is some relationship between these two places. Isn't it?'

'There must be a link of some kind.'

'Well, I need the closure report and any other information you can get.' Naveen hands him the case number.

'Okay, sir.'

Awasthi immediately goes to the section with all the storage cabinets. After some searching, he is able to find the required file and brings it to Naveen.

Naveen reads the report to see if the investigation conducted by the police or the investigating authority connect the accused to the crime being investigated. If not, then it is futile to prosecute the accused person.

'Awasthi, we can't go to the college without the permission

anyway, so let's go to Barabanki instead and see where Prakash used to live. We can also check if anyone there knows about Ansari and his background. Inform the area police station.'

'Makes sense, sir.'

'Also, if we see something, we'll ask Jayanti to file an appeal for her father's case. Take a picture of the file, and off the records, just cross-check the statements that people have given in the case. Why was there no concrete closure of the report? We may need to revisit the case,' says Naveen, still engrossed in reading all the information in the file.

'Sure, sir. Let's go.'

'Under which station does it come?'

'Mawai area, sir.'

'Okay,' he nods.

On their way to Mawai, Naveen looks tensed. Sensing Naveen's anxiety, Awasthi tries to lighten the mood. 'Sir, how's your brother, Raghav? Is he staying for a few more days or leaving? Please come to my home for dinner with Raghav?'

'He is staying here for a couple of more days. Thank you for the dinner invite, Awasthi. It's been long since I have eaten a decent home-cooked meal. Raghav and I will be honoured to be your guests.'

'Definitely, sir, Mrs Awasthi will be very happy to meet both of you.'

∞

Just when the police vehicle crosses the sign board on the left—Barabanki 0 km, Naveen asks, 'Awasthi, where is the force from the Mawai police station?'

'Sir, I had called SO sahab. He was supposed to reach here. I'll check with the police station.'

'No, you have informed him. That's enough. Let's go. Tell him to reach the location,' says Naveen and asks Awashti to drive to the location.

'Why is there such a huge crowd on the roadside, Awasthi? Is there any festival today?' asks Naveen, looking out of the window.

'Oh, sir, today is Bada Mangal. Bada Mangal is a unique festival of Lucknow. It is not celebrated in any other state or city, but it is celebrated with great pomp in and around Lucknow,' says Awasthi, navigating the vehicle slowly through the crowd.

'I've heard about it,' Naveen replies and nods.

'Yes, sir, in many homes, people do not cook at all. Everyone eats at these pandals serving food. You have to try it.'

'I'll try when we come back,' smiles Naveen.

'So, according to mythological beliefs, this festival is considered a symbol of the Ganga-Jamuni tradition of Lucknow. People of both Hindu and Muslim religions celebrate Bada Mangal.'

Awasthi accelerates to an optimum speed of 55 km/h on the highway and maintains the same.

'Also, sir, one day we should take a day off and go to Ayodhya.'

'Ayodhya? What brings this thought, Awasthi?'

'Sir, we are in the police, and once in a while, whenever we get a chance, we should visit a sacred place.'

Seventeen kilometres away, towards the Dullapur village, Mawai, the landscape changes like in a movie. The village is in a low-lying area, with a hot summer and chilly winter. As the car turns down a muddy road, the air feels fresh. The road to the village is lined with big trees on either side, and they are so green they look as if they are dancing with joy when the big trucks or buses pass by. There is a temple at the village entrance, where prayers and rituals are being conducted. There is a big hand pump near the temple surrounded by mango and neem trees and a big peepal tree behind the temple.

'We need to stop here, Awasthi, as per the location in the case file. This should be where Prakash used to live.' The big wooden bench under the neem tree catches his eyes even from a distance, and the stacks of sacks visible through the half-open door.

'Okay, sir,'

The vehicle stops, which draws the attention of all the people around. It's unusual to see a police vehicle in the village.

Naveen beckons to an old man resting on the wooden bench under the neem tree, awakened by the noise all around.

Looking at his uniform, the man says, 'What happened, sahab? Are you looking for anything?'

'What's your name?' asks Naveen, reaching him.

'Ramakant Yadav, sahab,' the old man says.

'Where does Prakash Shukla live?' Naveen asks the old man.

'No one lives here anymore. What happened, sahab?' Ramakant asks.

'Then who are you?' asks Awasthi.

'Sahab! I take care of this place. Last time Jayanti madam came, she asked me to continue to take care of this place,' replies Ramakant.

'Her father is my friend. I was out of station, so we were not in touch. I came here, so I thought of meeting him,' says

Naveen. A few people come and make a semi-circle around the wooden bench.

'Sahab, he is no more.'

'What happened to him?'

'It's almost a year, I think. He was a very good person. He was in the army and helped many people—from getting medicines from the government dispensary to applying for toilets in the village. Unfortunately, we lost him,' the old man says. 'I don't know anything, but some say he was involved with people who were into illegal business. God knows!' Ramakant pauses when he notices the others listening to him.

'Anything else you can tell us about Prakash? Any threat he was facing?'

'I am an old man, sahab. Don't drag me into it. I don't know anything else,' Ramakant begs.

'Do you know where Ansari lives?' requests Naveen.

'Who?'

'Shabaj Ansari is a professor in Lucknow,' Naveen tells him. Seeing no sign of recognition, he is about to fetch the picture from the college website, when Ramakant replies, 'Oh, Babban bhaiya?'

'Babban?'

'Yes, people call him Babban. Nobody calls him Shabaj Ansari here. That's his name in college,' the old man giggles.

'Okay. Do you know him? Where does he live?' enquires Naveen.

'At this time, he must be at his brick kiln.'

'Brick kiln? This is news!' says Awasthi looking at Naveen.

'Yes, he keeps visiting. He has a home in Lucknow and here also, so he stays here at times,' the old man says pointing towards the other side of the road.

'Okay. Thank you! Awasthi, let's go.'

Naveen and Awasthi head towards the south, a few kilometers away from here. On one side of the road, towards the west, one can see one village after another and on the east, which is just opposite the village, there are just green fields as far as one can see.

They can see smoke rising off the huge furnace, probably a kilometre from the road, towards the east. The brick kiln is in the center of the farm barricaded by a barbed wire from the left side. The right side is just open and ends at the Gomti River.

Thousands of migrant labourers, largely from the state of Odisha, come here to work in the brick kilns of Uttar Pradesh.

When they reach the kiln, Naveen and Awasthi notice a few women holding down pieces of coal with ungloved fingers and smashing them with a hammer.

'Sir, let's go this way,' Awasthi points towards the three one-storey concrete structures near the klin. There are big wooden tables laid out in the room but no sign of any activity or people.

Naveen nods and takes the lead, and Awasthi follows.

Men and women are walking barefoot towards the furnace as if climbing a pyramid. They are carrying freshly moulded bricks to the furnace. Labour laws and human rights are just a myth for them.

'Sir, nobody is here,' says Awasthi, peeping into the office.

'Wait!' says Naveen. Before enquiring about anybody or entering the office, they inspect the place and go to the backside.

They walk further and cross the huge stacks of fired bricks and walk towards the end where uncooked bricks are lying stacked.

Everything after here is strange. About 50 yards from them

towards the right, in the distance, is another godown-like place. The area is such that both of them are instantly on high alert. They want to make sure that they can catch Ansari in action here, so that they can take him in custody or for interrogation. There is a loud sound in the air, coming from the kiln itself—the furnace.

There is something oily and mesh-like stretching across the entire length of the land, starting from where they are standing.

'What's this smell?'

'Sir, maybe oil spill from a truck or something?'

'That's not the smell of oil, Awasthi.'

'Sir, they have burnt the leaves of the eucalyptus plant.'

Awasthi crosses a massive crater on the right, from where soil has been taken out for making bricks. He looks to Naveen, silently communicating with him. Naveen's eyes pull out a path where there is none.

Naveen goes first, crouching low, moving slowly towards the godown.

Naveen checks his scratched hand while walking in the brick kiln—there's a trickle of blood there.

Naveen pauses, as he feels he is being watched. He looks around him, but there's no one.

These two policemen keep moving forwards crouching low, keenly focused on the building to make sure that no one is coming out or going in. The mud is like oil, but they can feel something solid—like small glass bottles. Suddenly, a few of them crack under his boot with a loud crunch. Naveen and Awasthi are even more alert now.

They move quickly, pulling up the barbed wire up and crossing into a sugarcane field on the left. They throw themselves in and freeze because they hear someone talking about Ansari opening a new brick kiln. They must be workers at the kiln.

Naveen tells Awasthi to wait for his instructions in the sugarcane field. The godown is almost 50 yards from here. Naveen walks ahead.

The land is flatter here, and there is an eerie feeling of emptiness.

A short, dark man in his 50s emerges from the godown and waddles along the path. He must be younger than his appearance—he is wearing baggy slacks.

As Naveen turns the corner, he sees a tall man resting against the wooden pillar, a guava in his hand. His expression is one of utter disregard, as if he is merely waiting for something to happen. He looks like a factory worker. He isn't slumped at all—his body is clearly too muscular for that, yet it is just as relaxed as his face. He's almost smiling, as if something good is about to happen. A prickle of dread runs down Naveen's spine—something that is good for this man is likely bad for Naveen. Very bad.

A grey-haired man emerges from the building and nods at the tall man.

'What are you looking for?' asks the grey-haired man.

'Who is the owner of this brick kiln?' Naveen shouts, looking around.

A voice booms from afar, '*Kaun hai madarchod* (Who is it, motherfucker)?' Naveen notices a man engrossed in a game of chess alone in the corner, who gets up and starts approaching them, rubbing his beard.

'Khan sahab, looks like this policeman has lost his way,' the grey-haired man says.

'Who are you?' Naveen shouts at him.

Naveen and Khan look at each other. Khan nods. 'What happened, sir?' he asks. The voice is polite, but it sounds fake.

'Who are you and what are you doing here?' Naveen asks again.

'I am the owner of this place, Inspector, and I was playing chess there…and you came and disturbed all of us,' Khan says.

'You were playing chess alone?' Awasthi speaks.

'Babban always tells me to play alone—without an opponent. When I play chess from both sides, for every move I make, I have to fight for the next move. It's not difficult to defeat the other champion, if there, but when you have to fight against yourself, that makes you undefeated,' Khan smiles.

'You said you are the owner of this brick kiln? Are you?' Naveen asks. His anxiety is exploding.

'No, I am the partner in this brick kiln. Please tell me.'

'I need to search this place,' says Naveen.

'You can't do that. The temperature is very high inside right now. You can come after 15 days if you want, when the bricks are taken out of the furnace.'

'No, I need to check the place right now.'

'Sir, you won't be able to bear the heat. Workers in the past have fallen in the furnace and lost their lives. The kiln is built to retain heat and keep it as hot as possible. It's not safe for you.'

'Khan, please cooperate,' Naveen looks dead serious.

Khan listens intently. He moves closer. He stiffens, and when he speaks, his voice is low, threatening, 'Do you know, Inspector, how bricks are made and how they are hardened? Clay has a variety of different-sized particles. The smaller particles need less heat, and the tiniest of particles bond to the larger particles, making them hard. So, by cooking the brick in a kiln, you have made a tight collection of various-sized particles from a looser grouping of larger particles that are bonded together, making it strong. And with that brick, all these big buildings, hospitals, schools and even the police stations are constructed.'

Naveen spots a well-built young man stacking cardboard boxes. The ease with which he is working with the packages and stickers on the boxes shows that he is experienced at this work.

'There is nothing you will find here. So, it's better to go back now.'

'Where is Babban?' asks Naveen.

'He is not here. You can leave your number, and when he is back, he will call you,' says the man, frowning.

'I need to check this place,' says Naveen, and Awasthi walks a few steps towards him.

'Inspector, you should go back. You are unnecessarily troubling us. Many policemen come. They get their hafta. You will also get. Because everything has a price—good for good, bad for bad.'

'Are you trying to bribe me?' Naveen says, as he takes his gun out. 'No more tricks from you. I have got you now. Tell me who else is with you?'

'You don't know what you are doing, Inspector.'

'I know what I am doing very well,' Naveen walks to him, pointing the gun at his forehead. Naveen adds, '*UP Police hu behenchod! Pehle gand mein goli dalunga phir muh se sach nikalwaunga* (We're UP Police, motherfucker, we'll get the truth out of you).'

'You seem new to this, and you will lose your job, Inspector,' the man with the grey beard says.

But before anything else, Naveen needs to know what exactly is happening here, because this is no ordinary brick kiln. All this talk of high temperatures and Khan's threatening reaction has made it clear enough for him that something is amiss.

Naveen lowers his gun and jumps forward suddenly. Khan is startled, but before he or anyone else can react, he pushes Khan aside and rushes inside the klin. Once inside, his eyes widen at the sight—there are drums, tanks, suction machines, stacks and stacks of chemicals, water tanks, liquid food colour and a packing machine along with thousands of medicine bottles. This is clearly a chemical lab, and from the various items and the bottles, they are clearly manufacturing fake medicine.

Naveen is horrified. He is taking in the sight quietly, when the tall man grabs him by the collar and drags him out again. He whispers threateningly, 'If you don't stop messing around with us, then it will not be good for you, you know that.'

Naveen pushes away the tall man's hand and breaks free. He raises his gun again.

'We are just doing our business, so you mind your business,' Khan says.

'I know what kind of business you do. Your time is over,' Naveen says, pointing through the doors at the stacks of raw material.

Khan gives a smile and looks at his badge. 'Naveen Mishra, hmm…from where are you?'

'Khan, I don't have time for chitchat. You have to come to the police station with me.'

'Oh? I might not be as educated as you, but I also know a little bit about how the law works. Do you have a search warrant or an arrest warrant? What proof do you have that we do any illegal work? The white chalk is used for the education of our children. What's wrong with that?'

Khan keeps a hand on his shoulder and says, 'You know, the Gomti River is a few kilometres away from here, and the current is so intense that it is impossible to find the bodies of the people who drown in that river. You look like a good officer. Go and protect common people, they need your protection. Why are you wasting time here?'

'Are you trying to threaten me?' asks Naveen, furious.

'I am telling you how to stay safe. You are a young officer, but you are only powerful when you have this uniform on you. At the end of the day, you are just a servant with that badge of yours, and you are just a pawn for the masters to play with.'

All start laughing.

'Khan sahab, *thok dete hain madarchodon ko* (let's kill these motherfuckers),' one of the men shouts, brandishing a locally manufactured gun.

Naveen raises his gun again, and immediately the man fires a shot at him.

Naveen bolts, running close to the pillar for cover.

The gunfire alerts Awasthi, and he has the presence of mind to realize something is wrong. He jumps into the police vehicle and brings it towards Naveen. When Naveen comes running out of the kiln, he jumps into the vehicle, and they speed off.

The men chase them a little and fire a few shots in the air.

'Madarchod,' one of them shouts.

'Take me to the police station,' Naveen says.

∞

'Hello, Naveen,' says Deepak Verma, DCP (Central), Lucknow.

'Hello, sir, how are you? How come you are here today?' Naveen asks.

Deepak Verma was a subordinate of the superintendent of police, but when the department needed a DCP for Central Lucknow, Deepak Verma was the first choice because of his experience of more than 19 years in service.

'I was passing by, so thought of meeting Harsh Vardhan sir. So, how's your work going?' asks Verma. He adds, looking at Naveen's desk, 'What are you doing engrossed with these old files, Naveen!'

'Nothing, sir, just one of the cases. Coincidentally, one of your cases,' answers Naveen.

Verma looks at the file Naveen is holding, 'Oh! The Prakash Shukla murder case. This was my last case before I moved to the central office.'

'Sir, you are one of the sharpest officers. Then why did you close the case so quickly?' Naveen asks with concern.

'Being sharp does not mean you will solve each case you come across, Naveen. Sometimes, you need to close the file; otherwise, they roam around like a ghost,' says Verma. He sits on the chair at the other side of the table where Naveen is seated.

'I read the whole case; I feel the criminal is still roaming free.'

'What do you mean, Naveen?' Verma looks offended.

'Not to offend you, sir, but...'

'You are questioning my work. You have come here recently, and I have been working here for the last 19 years.'

'I am not questioning your work, sir.'

'You know nothing... You should be posted in some metro city.'

'Sir, of course, I have less experience than you, but I am just going by the books, and books never lie. The job of investigating any criminal case or matter rests upon the police in India. The police authority is responsible for investigating and finding evidence regarding a case against an accused person. This investigation carried out by the police must be conducted fairly and impartially. Article 21 of the Indian Constitution gives its citizens fundamental rights, which includes several rights such as Right to Food, Right to Shelter, etc., among which Right to Fair Trial and Investigation holds quite a crucial position as well. The 41st report of the Indian Law Commission recommended that an accused person should get a fair trial per the principles of natural justice. Efforts must be made to avoid delays in investigation and prosecution, and the procedures should ensure a fair deal for the poorer sections of society. A closure report, therefore, is a vital aspect of a proper investigation.'

'Whatever you say! I don't have time for your lectures,' says Verma and marches out of the office.

A medical assistant who has been waiting during this discussion comes forward. 'Sir, I need a blood sample,' he says.

'Why do you need my blood sample?' asks Naveen.

'Whose blood sample are you are matching it with?' jokes Awasthi.

'Sir, it's a regular body check-up of all the employees organized by the department,' responds the assistant while getting ready to take the sample.

'Okay, fine.' Naveen rolls up his sleeve, and the phlebotomist takes the sample from his arm.

'Done.'

He labels the sample and leaves.

twelve

18 January 2022. 11.00 a.m.

'Sir, look at these arrangements. We chose the wrong profession,' Awasthi says when the college gates open for the vehicle. The driveway is lined with triangular maroon flags. They wave in the breeze as Naveen and Awasthi drive towards the college building.

Naveen laughs, 'You bet.'

'They are in a lucrative business with an almost total market share of customers who can be easily influenced. All tax-free. Sir, do you believe in godmen or gurus?'

'Awasthi, "guru" is the purest and most dignified word. Even gods have gurus. However, some self-proclaimed people call themselves gurus and misuse the authority that comes with this appellation. Do you know that internal insecurities drive humans? They need somebody greater or on a higher pedestal than them to look up to for inspiration, hope or support to live a happy life, or at least the hope of having a good life. We want them and need them, hence they exist. The day we stop wanting them, they'll stop existing.'

'That's so true, sir.'

'It's also true that not all gurus are the same, as with policemen. Genuine people are rare and don't need a celebrity tag. Every person in this world has an agenda.'

'Sir, now they are very much active on social media as well, with millions of followers.'

'That's why they are invited and welcomed by the political parties,' smiles Naveen.

The police vehicle stops in front of the academic block to take permission from the dean before they enter the boys' hostel and question the students again about Ajay's death case.

Naveen enters the dean's office while Awasthi stands outside the office, listening to the conversation through the door. He can see Naveen's back through the glass window set in the door.

'Inspector Naveen, we can't make this college another case of those universities constantly raided by the police!' says the dean, sounding annoyed.

'Sir, we are here to investigate the case. Please try to understand.'

Naveen notices one button of the dean's shirt stands out—all the buttons are stitched in one pattern, but the one on his chest has a different design. It irritates him.

But before he can comment on it, the dean states, 'If you have permission or an order to investigate in the college, please submit that. I can't let you proceed otherwise.'

'What about having political rallies on the college campus?' asks Naveen, getting more and more irritated at the dean's uncooperative attitude.

'The order has not come from the high court yet that colleges or universities can't hold political rallies. There is only a petition filed to ban the political rallies, not the final order.'

'Sir, we just want to get done with the investigation. It's for one of your students.'

'That's what I am saying. The student is already dead, whether from suicide or murder. Why are you bringing down the reputation of the college? Do you understand that you are directly hampering the college's reputation? That too when there is a gathering of people here. Guruji is also coming today...'

'Sure, sir. I understand how much this means to you. I'll get the order and come back.' Naveen gets up from the chair.

'Sure.' The dean smiles and allows him to leave.

'Sir, get an arrest warrant against him and let's take him on remand,' says Awasthi, following Naveen to the vehicle.

'I wish we could, Awasthi. Most cases are stuck because of these bastards who don't let us work. Let's go to Guruji's place instead.'

'Guruji? Why suddenly, sir?'

'When I talked to the dean, I saw Guruji's photo frame in his office. The dean was offended when I asked about the investigation and his relations with Guruji. He would have handled it differently if he had been concerned about the reputation of the college. There is something we are missing here, Awasthi.'

'Sir, involving Guruji in this would be a little out-of-the-box. You know how it goes? He is a very well-known priest in Ayodhya. If anything comes out, it would cause us trouble. Anyway, local news channels and print media are just broadcasting so much about the racket.'

'Let's go and visit. As of now, we have no clue and nothing in our hands to investigate, so whatever information we can gather matters. Maybe it will help to connect the dots. Ajay was one of the bright boys.'

'Sir, should we inform DCP sir?' questions Awasthi.

'We'll inform him once we come back,' answers Naveen.

Awasthi remains silent.

Naveen continues, 'Don't worry, Awasthi.'

'Okay, sir.'

∞

Naveen and Awasthi are at Guruji's ashram, situated 30 kilometres from Lucknow towards Ayodhya, in civil dress. Awasthi parks the vehicle far away, and then they walk to the gate.

This is a yoga retreat, meant for those practising yoga, meditation and other spiritual practices. Such retreats are typically set outside a village or town in a quiet and peaceful locality. They consist of only basic facilities, with living quarters, dining hall, yoga hall, library and gardens.

'Hello, from how far you are coming here?' Awasthi asks a young man they pass by in the gardens.

'I didn't know about Guruji till June 2015. I was an atheist student, pursuing my PhD. As a scholar, I had a strong belief in research and science. I used to believe that science could do everything. Spirituality was a myth. People open these religious shops to loot gullible people in distress. But when I met Guruji, he changed my perspective on everything. You have come here to meet him for the first time?'

'Yes, officially, it's my first time, and I am also a student at the university. Glad to meet you,' Naveen says.

Unfortunately, their visit is in vain, as they find that Guruji has already left for his speech at the college.

∞

'Who do you think you are?' DCP Harsh Vardhan shouts. He is visibly angry.

Naveen does not speak.

'You are smart, intelligent and the youngest in the department. I am asking you a simple question. Who do you think you are?' the DCP asks him again.

'Sir, I am a servant of Uttar Pradesh Police.'

'Okay? And what's your duty?'

'To help people and help my peers and other officers to keep this city safe and crime-free.'

'Are you helping any of your peers except for Awasthi? Complaints are coming that you are misusing government resources.'

'Sir, I was about to share something with you. I did use the official vehicle but not for personal use.'

'I don't want to hear all that. All government servants must take an oath of service to the nation. Do you remember, Naveen? I took the oath when I became IPS and was appointed as DCP. We take the oath to be bound to that promise we made to serve the people. At times, it helps us a lot when we are unable to find the difference between right and wrong. I have made many wrong decisions, but I always made sure no harm came to my peers. Keeping them safe is also your responsibility.'

'Sure, sir. I'll keep this in mind.' Naveen is wondering what has put the DCP in such a foul mood. Their trip to Guruji's retreat didn't take long enough for the vehicle to be missed, that the DCP would get angry about that.

'Did you go to interrogate Guruji's associates in his ashram?' the DCP asks.

Naveen is standing in front of his wooden table, 'Yes, sir.'

'I know you are working on a case, but Naveen, Guruji is a respected personality, not just in Lucknow but in the state. Why the hell did you go to investigate there without any evidence or permission?'

So, this is what the issue is. 'Sir, there is something that the college dean is hiding,' states Naveen.

'Do you have any evidence?' asks DCP.

'No, sir. But I can find it.'

'Naveen, you don't have to be right every time and go chasing some hunch like this. If the police department wants it, it can make crime vanish from the country, but that's not the point. It would be best to ignore small problems to keep the country safe from bigger threats. Do you know the implications of your actions for the police department? You will not understand. Because you think solving a case will solve the whole nation's problems. You must be in the system if you have to keep things correct and clean. Patriotism is a great feeling, but it's only actionable when you are within the system. And what you are doing will only end in a letter of transfer, if not from me, from someone else. You have to understand that.'

'I do, sir. Still, I feel there is something big happening that we are not aware of. If you want me to change my strategy, I can do that. No problem,' replies Naveen.

The DCP nods. Then he suddenly asks, 'Naveen, how's your health?'

'Sir, I am fine.'

'Are you getting proper sleep? Are you facing any stress from this case or work?'

'No, sir. I am fine. I am working on the case, and soon, I'll have an update for you.'

'Okay. But Naveen, you are taking sedatives. I've just received your blood report, and a high amount of sedative has been found. You are risking your life and others' life. You have to stop working on the case immediately.'

'Sir, I am not taking sedatives. I am taking medication for some issues that I have been facing. It's nothing important.'

'That's just another form of the drug. Do you understand that? Even in that case, you should not be working on this case. I am sending you on paid leave for 15 days, so you can take a break. When you return, I'll have something else for you to work on. You will receive your suspension order from the CM's office.'

'Sir, I am very close to closing the case. I just need a few more days.'

'I am not asking for your suggestion. It's an order. Go! Take a break and take care of your health,' DCP Harsh Vardhan says.

When Naveen leaves, he sees Awasthi standing at the door, looking at him quietly.

∞

Ansari's house is decorated with framed phrases from the Holy Quran. It has understated but expensive furniture, which is neatly arranged.

It's quarter to 12 at night when Ansari quietly opens the

door to the bedroom where his son Asim is sleeping. He stands at the window that lets in the yellow glow from the streetlight into the room. The window has a clear view of the terrace of the guest house, where Raghav was staying. He pulls the curtains shut in one go. The room becomes darker. He sits on a chair next to Asim's bed and quietly picks up his cellphone. He gently takes Asim's index finger and unlocks the phone. He searches through the gallery until he finds the photo he is looking for and forwards it to his phone. He keeps the phone back in the drawer. This is a photograph of Raghav and Jayanti kissing each other on the terrace. He kisses Asim on the forehead and leaves the room, closing the door with a soft thump.

Ansari enters his own bedroom, the photograph open on his phone. His eyes are haunted, hungry. Holding the phone in his hand, he lies down comfortably on his bed. He stares at the photograph for a moment, then closes his eyes and lets his imagination go wild—he is thinking like any man who hasn't been with a woman for a long time.

He is unconscious of the little wild cries he utters at last. But it is over too soon.

thirteen

19 January 2022. 6.30 p.m.

It is dusk. The sky is cloudy and dark. It is always so in the late evening. This is the place where Jayanti has so many memories, and this is the place that has a lot of significance for both her and Raghav. A cold breeze is blowing, and the sun has set. The weather is pleasant.

'Kavu, I am leaving early and going to take a shower,' Jayanti says, panting after finishing the last round of the basketball match. She sits on the ground, wiping her face with a towel.

'Should I accompany you to the hostel?' asks Kavya, waving goodbye to the team.

'No, no, I am okay. I'll go, you carry on,' Jayanti says and walks out of the basketball court.

She is tired and drags herself down the shortest path through the academic block lobby, which connects to the hostel. The academic block has only one halogen light gleaming in the yard, and she feels scared, her fear of darkness rising in her. She wonders how the academic block is this big and yet left unguarded today. She calls Kavya. Though her phone rings, she does not answer.

She feels Kavya must have gone back to the court.

Her cellphone beeps with a new message on WhatsApp from an unknown number. When she sees it, she freezes, feeling the life draining out of her. It's a picture of her kissing Raghav on the terrace. The message says, 'the mole on ur neck, below the left ear, is just erotic.'

She tries to call the number, but the call cannot be placed. She takes the screenshot of the message, saves it in a private folder and deletes the WhatsApp message.

She gets a call. She thinks it's an unknown number, but it's Kavya.

'Hello?'

'Jayanti, have you seen that photo?'

Jayanti is shocked. 'Photo?' she mumbles.

'Yes! It's of you and Raghav on the terrace of the college guest house.'

At these words, Jayanti gets a sinking feeling in the pit of her stomach. 'Okay,' she manages to say.

'You come back to the hostel, and then we'll see what to do,' says Kavya, and disconnects the call.

The photo has already gone viral. So, deleting it from her phone will not help in any way. She tries the number again—same result. The number is not active for calling. She is shocked, but the photo is right there in front of her. She turns back towards the exit of the academic block from where she entered a moment ago. She is in complete shock, thinking of all the possible consequences of such a picture going public. Not only would there be action from the college, as they were on the terrace when they were not supposed to be, it would also affect her chances during placements. She doesn't know how to face this situation.

She feels the darkness around her and fears it will soon swallow her. Everything is messed up.

Jayanti calls Raghav immediately. When Raghav informs Naveen about the incident, Naveen asks both of them to come to the police station.

∞

Awasthi approaches Naveen when he sees him taking a pill from his drawer.

'Sir, how come you are here?' Awasthi asks surprised.

'You forgot me in a day, Awasthi...hmm...'

'No, sir. Just shocked. Sir, are you okay?' he asks, genuinely concerned seeing him taking the pill again.

'I am fine, Awasthi,' Naveen nods.

Awasthi does not say anything further but keeps looking at him. Naveen notices him and asks, 'What?'

'Nothing sir.'

'I am fine, Awasthi! These are just temporary,' he smiles and adds, '...and I am suspended but I can still come here, right! What will I do alone at home?'

'Of course, you can, sir.'

'Please let me know if you need anything.'

'Sir,' says Awasthi.

'Yes, Awasthi.'

'Sir, I wanted to say that the way you looked at me coming out from DCP's office, I wanted to say, I did not tell anybody anything.'

'I trust you, Awasthi. Relax!'

'Sir, you are anyway on leave, you should go somewhere

on vacation,' says Awasthi.

'I could, but then who will help them?' says Naveen, pointing towards Raghav and Jayanti entering the police station.

'Listen, you don't need to panic. You have the right to file an FIR. IPC, Section 354(C) of the Criminal Law (Amendment) Act, 2013, states that if any man captures or shares the image of a woman in a private space, they will be punished with imprisonment, which should not be less than one year and may extend up to three years and shall also be liable to fine. We can come to your college and start the investigation if you file an FIR. However, I am suspended for some reasons, but Awasthi can help you,' Naveen tells Jayanti and Raghav.

'Why are you suspended?' asks Raghav.

'That's a different story. Awasthi! Lodge an FIR,' Naveen calls. With two recent cases in the same college, Naveen feels confident of talking to DCP Harsh Vardhan about his suspension.

∞

Jayanti is on her way back from the police station. Her hair is flapping in the breeze, and her arms are tightly wrapped around her to protect her from the cold. Thinking about the photo, a few tears appear in the corners of her eyes. She wanted to meet her HoD, but his office was closed.

She walks past the lake, the guest house, and then the girls' hostel.

Jayanti sees Asim running towards her from the faculty house. His eyes are the same brown as his father's, and Asim is a year junior to her. For a long time, Asim had a crush on her, which he expressed a year ago. After that, Jayanti stopped talking to him.

Asim is not a favourite of Jayanti, but she keeps running into him at club events and other festivities in the college. He lives with his father in the professors' quarters, but at times, he stays in the hostel, where he has a single room, if he wants to stay with his friends.

'Hello, Jayanti ma'am,' Asim says, panting and wiping the sweat from his forehead.

'Hmm,' she responds.

His mouth is almost too dry to speak. He nods like an idiot and then croaks out, 'Ma'am, I saw something on WhatsApp. Sorry, ma'am. I wanted to say something.'

'What did you see on WhatsApp?' says Jayanti. Suddenly, all the dots connect. 'Fuck, you live right in front of the guest house—,' she adds in outrage.

'Ma'am, I respect you, and I've done nothing to hurt you,' Asim says. He's fidgeting, not able to look her in the eyes.

'Tell me! Did you click the picture and make it viral?' Jayanti is so angry that she can punch him in the face at any time.

'I am sorry. I clicked the picture but I did not share it with anybody.'

'What?'

At the breaking point of her patience, Jayanti lashes out at him, 'I thought you were not like others in the college, but now I know what you are, and your father will explain this to the dean and the police.'

'Ma'am, I offer prayers five times a day. I swear on Allah and the Quran, I have not done it. I may have lied before, but I am not lying to you now. I just came here to help you, and I will confess.'

At this, Jayanti punches him in the face. He almost falls

to the ground, wailing in shame.

She holds his collar and says, 'Do you know what you have done? You are gone now.' She drags him by his arms towards the dean's office.

'Ma'am, please, it will ruin my career and my father's job. I want to go abroad for further studies. Please, ma'am!' he begs.

'Fuck you! And fuck your father. I have already filed an FIR, and they will soon come and ask you.'

Her face is red with suppressed rage, which is rushing through her body like deathly poison.

'I would have done the same if I was in your situation. I'm ready to confess and help you in whatever way I can.'

∞

It's 9.30 p.m. Asim reaches home, horrified and disgusted. He goes to his father's room and says, 'Abbu, I want to share something with you.'

'Yes, son, what happened? Why do you look so worried?' asks Ansari.

'Abbu, I used to like a girl from fourth year, and one day, I clicked a picture of her, but I don't know, now it's gone viral in the college. I am so scared, Abbu. Those who know will suspect me only.'

'Asim! You should have told me about this before. Now, don't tell anyone else about it. Your application for transfer to another campus is already processed, so keep quiet,' Ansari tells him.

'Okay, Abbu.'

fourteen

20 January 2022. 6.00 a.m.

Jayanti is suddenly woken up by a call from Raghav. She sits up to take the call. 'What happened? Have you left?'

'No, I am staying at a hotel in the city. Naveen asked me to stay back. Also, I wanted to stay back for you. Listen! Naveen wants to enter college. Can you help him?' says Raghav.

'What? Why does Naveen want to come to the college at this hour? Is it about the FIR? But he is suspended, right? Listen, please don't create any more trouble for me now.'

All Jayanti feels right now is a desire for this whole episode to end. She just wants to get placed at a good company and get away from this college, the place of so much pain.

'You can trust me, Jayanti. I'll tell you everything in detail. I am standing near the main gate with him,' says Raghav.

'Oh god! You could have told me earlier that you were coming. Okay, listen! Don't stand near the main gate; you are not a guest now. Moreover, you are with a police officer. So, guards will quickly notice you, especially at this time.'

'We are in funky college attire. We'll manage the guards, don't worry.'

Naveen, who is standing beside Raghav, tells him that there are no cameras at the gate. Raghav confirms with Jayanti. Awasthi, wrapped in the muffler, is observing the situation from the police vehicle.

'There are no cameras, but please be careful. Do one thing, go ahead and reach the new gate. Just walk straight from the main gate around 200 meters. I'll come there.'

The college is located on the national highway, and most people around that area are college students or staff members of the college.

'You are terrible at acting like a student. You have to look like you belong here,' says Raghav.

'Yes, I know,' says Naveen nervously. This is a new experience for him, since he is used to going everywhere as a policeman. Raghav is fiddling distractedly with his phone, waiting impatiently for Jayanti to turn up, when he sees her approaching him from the direction of the main gate they just walked past.

'We can go when the new guard comes on duty. It may be risky going in now,' Jayanti says, coming up to them.

'What should we do now?' asks Naveen.

'Nothing. Just come with me. Just be casual. Don't overact.'

They reach the gate. This gate is always closed.

'The new guard doesn't ask questions, and it's better than jumping over the wall. If you get caught, there is no second chance.'

They can see the guard standing at the gate. He seems to be watching something on this phone. Jayanti approaches him and asks, 'Bhaiya, ATM is working?' The ATM is attached to the college gate.

'Yes,' says the guard, returning to his cellphone.

'Thank you, bhaiya,' responds Jayanti and goes into the ATM.

After two minutes, she comes out and tells him. 'It's not working. Can you check?'

The guard looks irritated at having to pause his video. He goes into the ATM. Jayanti signals Raghav and Naveen to enter the college while the guard is inside.

It's a cold winter morning, and the sun is still resolutely below the horizon. The street is as dark as in some old black-and-white movies, with the street lamps casting pools of light at intervals. But gradually, the sun will take over from the lamps and everything will be bathed in sunlight.

They cross the fountain and take a left towards the grounds, strewn with chairs post the Guruji's visit. They stop there.

BZZZ! Naveen's phone rings, breaking the silence, and he quickly fishes it out and answers.

'Sir, I have an update on the FIR Jayanti madam registered,' says Awasthi.

'Awasthi! We have to focus on Ajay's case first.'

'But sir, you asked me to track down the WhatsApp number. So, I got the details you wanted.'

'Because that's how I could enter the college, with the help of Jayanti and Raghav. Now, let's focus on this,' says Naveen.

'But I have something to share with you,' pauses Awasthi.

'What, Awasthi?'

'We can't access the encrypted WhatsApp messages or calls. For that, we need high-end software. However, yesterday, when Jayanti came to the police station, we logged the FIR, and then Raghav and Jayanti left. After an hour, she had come back, as she remembered something, but you were not there. She mentioned Ansari's son, Asim, who is also studying in IEC. Just to be on the safer side, and just because he is Ansari' son, I got the call details of his number unofficially. And one number is frequent in his incoming call list: it's from labour who works in Ansari's brick kiln. But that's not all. Professor Ansari has 100–200 acres of land in Barabanki worth rupees 50–80 crore.'

'What? Are you joking, Awasthi?' Naveen is in shock.

'No, sir. I trust my sources. It's true.'

'Awasthi! Don't share this with anyone. I am not on duty. Let me just find a way to talk to the DCP.'

'Sir, I got the whole history of the professor. Ansari is from Barabanki. For all others, he is a professor, but in reality, he is a businessman. He has multiple properties in the name of his family members and relatives. In 2013, money suddenly started flowing into his account. I'll text you his income details. He was never caught because this is all white, but I am sure there will be something shocking when we deep dive into it. That's not all. There were some FIRs a couple of times from locals, but later, neither did the victims appear nor were the complaints processed further. All the FIRs were closed, year after year. He is as clean as filth. This is a mystery for you to solve. Before being appointed professor at IEC, he had a pharmacy store in his village, which was running at a loss. Later, he completed his PhD from Kharagpur at one of the prestigious institutes.'

'Awasthi! This is massive information. Thank for you this. However, none of this makes him guilty of any crime.'

'Hmm, that is true,' agrees Awasthi.

Naveen's subconscious mind starts counting the trees on both sides of the path. In the light of the rising sun, they cast long shadows. He starts calculating the height of the trees based on this.

'What are you thinking?' says Raghav, watching his expressions.

This breaks Naveen's reverie.

Raghav, Naveen and Jayanti are standing in a triangle at the end of the ground. Some dismantled old machines and bits are piled into a heap, and others can hardly notice them here at this hour.

'Nothing! Can you take me to the hostel?' Naveen asks Jayanti.

'At this time! We will be noticed easily because no one gets up so early. Let's wait for the mess to open for students,' suggests Jayanti.

Naveen nods. 'Where does Asim live?' he asks.

'In the faculty houses over there,' answers Jayanti, pointing.

'I know a place to hide...' Raghav says.

'Where?' asks Jayanti.

'That place behind the cafeteria, where we went?' replies Raghav.

She nods.

They walk until they see a cluster of small trees behind the fountain. A few more yards, and they reach a desolate area at the extreme end of the campus. The entire landscape is covered with rubbish. Old furniture lying around, empty, collecting dust. The street lamps throw little circles of white light on to an empty, cracked sidewalk.

'Is this a chemistry lab?' asks Naveen, his face disgusted.

They walk towards an old laboratory adjacent to the construction site, now a tomb of rubble and dirt.

'It's not functional,' responds Jayanti.

He nods.

Raghav sniffs, remembering the smell from when he came here with Jayanti a few days ago. It's stronger today, and he is able to identify it better. 'There is a sweet chemical smell here, as if someone is doing a Benzene test in the lab,' he says.

'The chemical lab is on the other side, and workers must be working on the construction site,' Jayanti explains.

'Let's go back. The place is filthy, to say the least. Curiosity is out of the question, and no sane person would come here except for business or to hide,' says Raghav, holding his nose.

'Wait!' Naveen walks ahead.

'What are you doing?' asks Jayanti and then looks at Raghav to stop him before anyone else notices him.

Naveen is following the patches of white cement on the ground. When they reach the old lab, the stench hits them first—a mixture of something rotten, something dead. A few workers getting ready to start the day's work notice him. They call out to him, asking him to go back because of the construction site's cement dust.

But Naveen knows he is on to something. He bends over to collect a handful of white powder from the ground and keeps it in the plastic pouch he takes out from his pocket. He places some of it on his palm and tastes it, spitting it out immediately.

'What is he doing?' asks Jayanti, amazed.

'Police officers are like that, I guess?' Raghav mumbles, also confused.

'Really?' she sighs. 'We really shouldn't be here.'

Naveen turns back. He is in a hurry, his expression serious, 'I need to leave. Can you show me the exit?'

'Why are we in such a hurry? And wait, you wanted to go to the hostel na?' asks Jayanti to both of them.

Raghav has no clue.

'Yes, but right now we just need to leave. I'll call you if I need help. Thank you so much, Jayanti.'

She nods and gives a forced smile. Naveen and Raghav head towards the gate.

∞

'What happened, sir? Anything to be concerned about?' asks Awasthi, ready to start the vehicle and drive at his command.

When Naveen doesn't respond, Awasthi asks again, 'Is everything fine, sir?'

'Nothing is going fine, Awasthi. Can you take me to the KGMC hospital? I know someone who may help me at this hour.'

Naveen sits in the front while Raghav gets in the back seat.

'Sure, sir.'

'Raghav, if I am correct. This is not the fucking Benzene smell. These students don't know they are sitting on a volcano.'

'What do you mean?' a shocked Raghav asks Naveen, looking in the rear-view mirror.

'You must know that supplying counterfeit medicines is at its peak in the state. A few weeks ago, the UP Special Task Force, in a joint operation with Foods Safety and Drug Administration, recovered a stock of counterfeit medicines in Barabanki. This is all connected and finally making sense to me.' After a pause, he calls out, 'Awasthi! WhatsApp me the pictures of Ajay's file and his post-mortem report.'

'Okay, sir.'

∞

It's 7:30 in the morning when Dr Shaina's cellphone rings. The cellphone displays Naveen's name, and Dr Shaina quickly picks up the call.

In a sluggish voice, she answers, 'What happened, Naveen? Is everything fine?'

'Everything is fine. I wanted some help,' Naveen says.

'It's my day off, Naveen. I'll call you in the afternoon. Look at the time,' Dr Shaina adjusts the soft ruffles in the grey satin of her mid-length nightdress and goes back to her bed silently while her boyfriend turns to the other side of the bed.

'I can't wait till afternoon, Shaina!' says Naveen urgently.

'You know, because of you, my boyfriend thinks I am having an affair with someone—all these calls at odd hours.' She walks to the balcony of her bedroom.

'About that I can talk to Amit, if you like. I am so sorry, but it's urgent. I need a favour from you, and it's important.'

'Tell me.'

'I am reaching KGMC. I have something with me, and I want you to tell me its contents.'

'I did not get you.' Dr Shaina is confused.

'There was a post-mortem report from the hospital for one of my cases, Ajay, a few weeks ago. The report mentioned that he consumed a drug that had no medical impact on his body.'

'So?' she asks.

'So, I want to confirm if that content is the same as what I have with me.'

'You mean, sample match?'

'Yes.'

'Naveen, I am a surgeon by training and a psychiatrist by profession, neither a lab technician nor in the post-mortem department.'

'That I know. But can you help me, Shaina? Please!' Naveen requests her.

'Okay, I can connect you with a friend. Her name is Deepali. She is an MBBS and not a forensic medicine specialist nor into post-mortem examinations, but I am sending you her number. She can help you. But don't call her right away. Let me talk to her first.'

'Sure. Thank you so much.'

'You owe me a treat for this.'

'I do. Thanks!'

∞

Naveen, Raghav and Awasthi are on the Faizabad–Lucknow highway in the police jeep, speeding at 65 km/h, on their way to the King George Medical College.

'Can't you switch off these red and blue lights?' Raghav asks Awasthi.

'Fuck, I hate these flashers. But I can't do that right now,' Awasthi says.

A typical day in KGMC begins at 8 a.m. for MBBS students, so-called Georgians.

Raghav and Naveen find the back entrance of the KGMC hospital and wait for Deepali to come out and meet them.

Unexpectedly, Naveen notices a man with a dark complexion standing across the road, staring at them for the last few minutes. He is about six feet tall with a medium build and has a moustache. He looks old, but is perhaps between 30 and 35 years in age. He is wearing dirty blue jeans, a white, short-sleeve T-shirt with a logo on the back and dirty white sports shoes. He runs out of the street with a brown bag in his left hand. As he runs, he carries his right arm across his chest as if it's in a sling. Naveen, immediately suspicious, starts chasing him. The man begins walking faster towards the narrow streets opposite the hospital back gate before he disappears. Naveen starts running behind him, and catching up to him, grabs him by the shoulder.

'Motherfucker! Who are you?'

'Sorry, sir, I have not done anything. Please leave me. I have not done anything. I'll not come here. Please, sir.'

'Why were you running? How did you get these wounds on your neck?'

Naveen holds his collar tightly. He almost chokes.

'Who are you? Show me your ID. Else, I'll lock you up right now.'

The man does not show anything and shivers in fear. Naveen grabs his pocket and discovers multiple IDs.

Just then, Raghav and Awasthi catch up.

'What is this?' Naveen asks the man.

'I am a bangle seller. My name is Abdul. I am sorry. I know it's illegal to carry multiple IDs, but there is no other way to earn my bread and butter. They asked about my religion, and I was beaten by some men because I was not allowed to come near Hindu women. They said they would hand me over to the police with the charges that I was influencing Hindu girls. Love jihad, they said. So, I created an ID with a Hindu name to hide my identity.'

'Then why were you running?' Awasthi asks him.

'I got scared, sir. I am sorry.'

'Where are you from?' Naveen asks, giving him a five-hundred-rupee note. He adds, 'Go and take medicine.'

'Sir, my family lives in Mawai, a small place near Barabanki.'

'We need to go, sir. Deepali ma'am must be waiting for us,' Awasthi tells Naveen.

'Don't run after seeing the police. *Koi thok dega, behenchod, raat mein aise bhagega toh* (You'll get yourself killed, motherfucker, if you run like this at night).'

'Okay, sir.'

∞

The hospital was built long ago, like the city that surrounds it. Outside, the streets are wide and straight. Inside the hospital, the hallways are the same, wide enough. Whoever the architect was, there was a clear plan. The British did an excellent job of establishing this great institution in Uttar Pradesh that offers medical help to many cities.

'Hello, Naveen?' a woman calls out to him, wearing a doctor's coat while they are standing at the corner of the gate.

'Hello, Dr Deepali?' he asks.

'Yes, Shaina told me about you.'

'Thank you so much for helping, Doctor,' says Naveen.

'No problem. Give me the sample, but it will take some time.'

'How much time it will take?' asks Naveen.

'I won't be the one doing the test. I'll ask someone to do that. But remember, it's on Dr Shaina, so I hope you keep this with you only. You can wait or go. It will take 30 minutes to an hour.'

'Sure. We can wait here till then,' Naveen says and looks at Awasthi and Raghav.

'Okay. I'll keep you posted. If you want, you can wait in the cafeteria or near the OPD,' Dr Deepali suggests.

Naveen gives Dr Deepali the sample of the white powder he collected from the college. She takes it and heads off towards the hospital.

∞

Naveen lights a cigarette and takes a long puff, stubbing it within moments. The tip of the cigarette burns violently as he sucks on it. There is some tension on his forehead. They are sitting on the bench at the small tea stall next to a pharmacy. Its green light glows into the new day, illuminating the street like fresh springtime leaves.

'*Do chai*,' says Naveen.

'*Ji, sir*,' responds the tea-stall guy.

'Raghav?' calls out someone with a chirping voice. Raghav is stunned for a moment and turns, worried about who has seen him with Naveen.

'Archana ma'am!' he gives a big smile.

'What are you doing here?' she asks and looks at Naveen, 'Hello,' she adds.

'Nothing. He is my cousin, an SP in UP Police.'

'I see. Glad to meet you. Must be a tough time for UP Police,' she smiles. Naveen nods at her in greeting.

'Such a pleasure meeting you after so long,' Raghav says as he offers her tea.

'Thank you.'

Raghav met Archana when he attended the Lucknow Literature Festival. She is an enterprising journalist and thrives on influencing and persuading others.

He adds, 'How come you are here? Is everything all right?'

'Oh yes, I had come with the team. The Cabinet Minister is admitted here, so had a visit.'

'And what brings you all here?' she questions in return.

'I know someone admitted here, so we came to see him,' he replies.

'You are working with News24, right?' asks Raghav curiously.

'Yes, that's the place where you will find me. Let me know if you need any help.'

'Sure.'

'Well, I'll leave. See you.'

∞

After waiting for an hour, Naveen gets a call from Dr Deepali. She asks him to come to the first floor laboratory next to the OT.

They reach the first floor in no time. Dr Deepali is waiting outside the laboratory.

'I have something interesting to share with you,' she says, leading them inside. 'This test is a no test.'

'What do you mean?' asks Naveen, confused.

'This test does not show any specific results. This is simple $CaCO_3$, which is nothing but calcium carbonate. Here is your report,' explains Dr Deepali. 'I am sure you were expecting this, so why do you look stunned?' she asks, seeing the shock on his face.

'Shit! I was not expecting this at all. Can I talk to you for a minute?' Holding the report in his hand, Naveen asks her to step out into the corridor outside the laboratory.

'What's the matter?' Dr Deepali asks.

'Mafias are handling the racket of counterfeit medicines across the country from Barabanki. They are freely running this racket. This is being supplied to the whole country from Barabanki, and they have at least millions of counterfeit doses. This is the only evidence I have to track down the racket. Can you tell me anything else that can help?'

'Naveen, even if this is being used to produce counterfeit medicines, you will have a hard time proving it until you test each tablet in the laboratory. This content will never cause death; it is just a straightforward dose of calcium carbonate. The recommended amount for most adults is 1,000–1200 mg per day. Therefore, if you typically consume two to three tablets of it, it will not cause any problem for anybody; 500–600 mg of calcium carbonate you can take daily. And chalk is the most common natural form of calcium carbonate.'

'Okay…' says Naveen pensively.

'And counterfeit medicines are not new to us. We have done the tests in the past, but usually, these were for cases where nicotine mimics a chemical needed to make the nerves function. Thus, it brings a chemically induced "rush". Then the body adapts and makes less of the natural chemical. Essentially, natural chemicals plus nicotine equals the level a non-smoker has. To get another rush, the smoker would need to increase the nicotine and smoke more…But their body adapts again and reduces the amount of the natural chemical in the bloodstream. If the smoker stops smoking or reduces consumption, their nerves cease to function normally, and they feel "jittery", as they no longer make enough of the natural chemical on their own. So, when you take medicine and feel better, next time, even if you have a less severe symptom of a viral, you have the urge to get the same medication by default because you feel a little better. And that's how the counterfeit medicines business work, mostly in small cities and towns. In simpler words, you become addicted to these medicines.'

'Thanks, doctor. Thank you for the help,' Naveen keeps the report with him and leaves with Awasthi and Raghav.

fifteen

20 January 2022. 10.00 a.m.

Back at the police station, Naveen requests DCP Harsh Vardhan to join him in the conference room that they use for meetings. Awasthi is already present with a projector, with the screen installed.

Awasthi switches on the projector as soon as Naveen and the DCP enter the room.

'Yes, tell me Naveen,' says the DCP, taking a chair.

Awasthi closes the door. Naveen starts, 'Sir, this is Ajay's post-mortem report. This is a powder we got from the college; there were boxes and small bottles in that area. Unfortunately, we could not get a picture. However, there is one thing common in all three places. The powder content found in Ajay's body was calcium carbonate. The powder we got from the college is calcium carbonate, and the boxes and glass bottles we saw in a brick kiln in Barabanki, also calcium carbonate—these three are somehow linked with each other; as you always say, "tightly coupled". The boxes and small glass bottles are usually used for medicines and syrups.'

'Whose brick kiln it is?'

'Professor Ansari.'

'Who is he?'

'A professor from IEC, the same college where Ajay was found dead; the powder was found near a construction site within the campus.'

'What the fuck!'

'Yes, sir.'

'So, you mean Shabaj Ansari is involved in it?'

'Awasthi...' Naveen motions towards Awasthi to proceed with the update.

'Sir, Ansari is from Barabanki. He is a professor at IEC, but in reality, he is a businessman with multiple properties in the name of his family members and relatives.'

'Having properties in the name of family members may cause doubt but does not prove him guilty of anything,' the DCP says.

'True, sir. He is not guilty. He is a good man in front of some people. He donates money to the low-income families for their daughters to get married. That makes him a local hero. You never know, if he stands for an election, he might win. Well, there were some FIRs against him which were closed, year after year. In the Prakash Shukla murder case, if you study the whole case, the prime suspect should have been Shabaj Ansari, who was the last person with the victim before the assassination happened. However, his name was never in the list of suspects. Deepak Verma was in charge of the case.'

'Yes, I know that Deepak was handling the case, but how do you know so much about that case? That case is already closed.'

'Yes, sir. That case was closed, but Shabaj Ansari and Prakash

Shukla were friends. Then what happened was that Prakash was murdered. If Ansari was not involved in this, and he was the last person to see Prakash, his statement should have been recorded, but there is no such statement in the case file. Sir, either we have a loophole in the department or we need to look into the case again. That's all I have. Thank you.'

Awasthi goes back to his seat, while the DCP remains silent, and Naveen waits for him to speak.

'This is all great, but I have already appointed Verma to Ajay's case. If you want, you can share the pieces of evidence with him,' DCP Harsh Vardhan tells Naveen.

Standing on the other side of the table, Naveen says, 'When I was in school, my father used to say, I quote, "*kahani mein jis bhi kirdar ka naam sabse jada baar aaye, kahani ka asli hero wahi hota hai* (The real hero of the story is the one whose name comes the most number of times in the story)." In this story, you will find my name from the crime scene till here. Rest, I'll do whatever you say. Anyway, I am on paid leave, sir!'

'There is a process for an investigation, Naveen. If you don't follow the process, who else will in the department? Then run this police station like a fish market!'

'I did not mean it in that way, sir.'

'From where did you get all this information, evidence, report, etc?'

'I am sorry, sir, I can't reveal my sources, but I can assure you that if you bring me back into the investigation, I can bust the whole racket.'

'Like this? You will handle the whole situation like this? You both don't share updates with anyone, and you don't discuss things with me either,' DCP Harsh Vardhan looks at Naveen and then Awasthi. Awasthi remains silent and gives him a fake awkward smile.

'I was on suspension, sir, so I thought it wise not to disturb you,' responds Naveen.

'Don't give me that excuse. You were already working on the case. Well, from tomorrow, you are back on the case, but I need to be updated about all goings-on. You are a smart officer. I have no problems with you, but you still have to learn a lot many things,' says DCP Harsh Vardhan.

'Sir, but my suspension order...' Naveen says.

'I'll take care to revoke the order. Also, I need the update on the case in my office tomorrow. You may leave.'

'Thank you, sir.'

∞

Asim is huddled up alone in a cell. After a beat...the doors ratchet open, and he stares into the shadows. There's a single table and two chairs inside the cell. It's a plain room with spartan furniture, nothing close to what is shown in the movies. The walls have no soundproofing, and it does not muffle the screams at all. The chairs are chained or bolted to the floor, as is the table.

Naveen sits down and keeps his cellphone on the table to record the conversation.

'Do you know why you are here, Asim?' Naveen asks, looking at Asim, observing him closely.

'I have no idea why I have been called here, and I was anyway about to go to another campus of IEC under the scheme of inter-transfer of students,' Asim says clearly.

'That's one of my questions, but I'll come to that later.

My first question is, how long have you known Jayanti?' asks Naveen, joining his hands on the table.

'I know her from the very first year of college. We belong to the same youth club, so…'

'Okay. Did you know that she was in a relationship with someone or if she had an affair?'

'Yes, Raghav.'

'Did you click the picture of Raghav and Jayanti on the terrace?'

Asim hesitates, not saying anything.

'You have already confessed to Jayanti about it.'

Asim nods.

'Okay, good. I want you to speak the truth, which will help me keep you away from all this. You are a good boy, aren't you?' He must know by now that he has committed a crime under the Indian Penal Code, Section 354(C).

'Okay,' Asim responds.

'Did you know that Jayanti has feelings for you, but she has never told you?' Naveen is now in shady territory, but this emotional card always works for the youth.

'But…she never said that,' says Asim.

'Because she was always afraid of how your father would react. So, she did not say anything.'

'But how is this interrogation related to what she thinks about me?' he says, suddenly suspicious.

'Because your father is a prime suspect in her father's murder case. She is afraid of him, but she likes you, so she never said anything against your father. You know, "Love quotient". Anyway, that case is closed, so no problem.' *This should make him feel safe with me*, Naveen thinks.

'Okay,' Asim nods and takes a sip of water from the glass on the table.

'How much do you know about your father, Asim?'

'He is the ideal father. He is loving, caring and always thinks of my future.'

'Hmm, okay. Do you know that he is involved in the business of fake medicines?'

'What! I don't know anything about it.'

'You never heard any conversation of your father with anybody or noticed anything weird about him?'

'No!'

'Asim, you have to think twice before saying anything because if you speak the truth, it can save all of you. Do you understand that?'

'Yes, I do, but I am not lying.'

'Okay, no problem. Did you have a hand in making the photograph of Jayanti viral?'

'No. I offer prayers five times a day. I swear on Allah and the Quran, I have not done it. I just came here to help you, and I will confess if I have done anything.'

'Asim, in all the cases in court, both the parties take a sacred oath to speak the truth, but one party is telling a lie, isn't it? So, you are okay if I check your phone or call records,' says Naveen.

'You are absolutely free to do that. I have nothing to hide,' says Asim confidently.

'Okay. Fine, you can go now. I'll call you back in case I need your help. Thank you, Asim,' Naveen keeps a hand on his shoulder, a gesture to earn his trust.

'Thank you.'

∞

'Sir, what were you doing there in the lock-up?'

'Awasthi, what's the progress on Ajay's case?' Naveen enters his office and asks Awasthi. 'Did you recover anything from his room? Anything that could lead us to Ansari and his son Asim? Can you show me the file?'

Awasthi again goes to the records and property room, which is a secure storage area for case files and evidence. A technician manages all the submitted property (evidence) by packaging, cataloguing and storing them. Awasthi searches the files from the recent stack and hands them over to Naveen.

Naveen goes through the file again—all the evidence, the post-mortem report, photographs, family background of the victim and the sketch of the crime scene and victim.

'Awasthi, did we make the sketch of his room as well?'

'No, sir.'

'Okay. Was his room searched at least?'

'Yes, there was nothing recovered from his room but an empty bottle of Formol and a pair of gloves from the dustbin. There were no fingerprints on it, there was no significant evidence. It's there in the report.'

Naveen checks the file once again and starts examining the crime scene sketch.

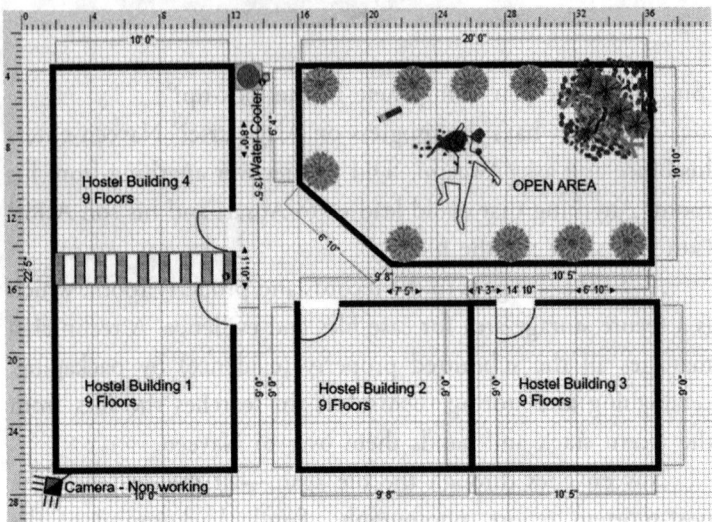

'Also, sir, I am not 100 per cent sure, but I have something important to share with you,' Awasthi says in a rush. Naveen closes the file and asks, 'What happened, Awasthi?'

'Guruji, you know. He is a trustee of IEC.'

'What do you mean?' Naveen is taken aback at this turn of events. His brain is immediately trying to link all the events based on this new information.

'Guruji provides funds to the college, and the college uses these same funds to invite companies to the college for placement. No doubt the college produces good students, but that's how the college has such a big name and high number of placements.'

'What's wrong in that? Even if the college is paying the companies to come, it doesn't matter because it's for the betterment of the students.'

'Yes, but in return, the dean promotes Guruji among students and does his branding. Did you notice that at any event at the college, the chief guest is always Guruji? Because of this, the media ends up presenting Guruji as a guru of the entire state. There is something more than the events and donations to the college. You must look at that side as well.'

'How did you come to know this?' Naveen asks.

'I have my sources. But what should we do now? Should we talk to DCP sir?' Awasthi asks.

'I don't know. Maybe not yet.'

∞

Asim reaches home, panting, opens the cupboard in the kitchen and dials a number from another phone.

'Brijesh Chacha, police had called me for interrogation. You have to stay alert and tell papa also. He never listens to me.'

There's pause while he listens to the person on the other side.

'No, I have not spoken, but that police officer tried everything to get me to speak, but I did not give in.'

Another pause.

'I know, Chacha. Also, Chacha, they may be tapping all the personal numbers for surveillance.'

Asim nods vehemently at something Brijesh Chacha says. 'Okay, Chacha! Bye.'

Asim disconnects the call, wraps the phone tightly in a polybag, goes to the bathroom, pulls up the flush tank cover and tapes the packet there.

sixteen

20 January 2022. 2.00 p.m.

Jayanti is waiting by the giant billboard on the side of the road. She sees the police vehicle approaching down the Lucknow–Faizabad highway towards Barabanki, headlights on full beam.

The vehicle stops in front of her.

'Hey, come inside,' Naveen says, seated at the steering wheel.

Jayanti opens the back door and gets in. 'What happened? Why did you want to meet me at this hour?' she asks.

'I wanted to tell you something about your father's murder case,' Naveen says and parks the vehicle on the side of the road.

'Yes, please,' she shifts to the left so that she can clearly see Naveen talking.

'And I want you to help in the investigation.'

'Of course, I'll do that,' she affirms.

'We suspect that Ansari was involved in your father's murder case.'

'What? No! My father and Ansari were good friends, and nothing could make him a murderer. I can't believe it. Do you mean he killed my father?' She just stares at Naveen wide-eyed, like the whole world is crumbling around her.

'That we are not sure of as of now. He is not guilty yet, but we suspect him. The pieces of evidence we have, the logic Awasthi and I have followed, all point to him.'

'Have a look at this,' Naveen hands an old file to Jayanti.

'What's this?' asks Jayanti.

'This is the last case file your father worked on before he left the police department in 2019. The case was about a land dispute, and the allegation was that Ansari had illegally captured the place. The case went to court, and Ansari won the case. A week later, the victim's mother's body was found in the river. There was an internal enquiry against your father and the department. We don't know what happened after that.'

'You mean, my father was involved with Ansari?'

'We don't know that, but all these events mean there was some connection between your father and Ansari. We'll find out.'

She stays silent for some time and then says, 'Ansari was with the police officers all the time during the investigation of my father's death—' Her legs start shaking, and her hands start feeling cold. She feels suffocated.

Naveen holds her hands, 'Jayanti, I understand your pain. But we need you to help get some information, so you have to remain calm.'

'I'll try,' says Jayanti, taking a few deep breaths. 'So, what about the photograph of Raghav and me that went viral in college, do you mean Ansari did that too?'

'You mentioned that Asim clicked the picture in desperation, so anyone of them could have done that. We'll soon figure it out.'

'Okay, so what do you need my help with?'

'You have to take me to your place. I need to search your home. Then you have to take me to Ansari's house in the village. How frequently does he go to his house in the village anyway?'

'He used to come on weekends. Not sure about these days.'

'Okay. How long has Ramakant been working for your father?'

'How do you know him? Did you go to my place? Ramakant uncle is like my grandfather, he is taking care of the farms and our home after my father. He is the only trusted person I know.'

'Yes, I went there, but Ramakant did not speak much about your father or Ansari or anything that could give us a lead in the case.'

'Okay, I'll take you there whenever you want to go.'

'Thanks.'

Naveen starts the vehicle and accelerates towards Dullapur to reach Mawai village.

'Sir, do you know the story behind the famous Parijat tree in Barabanki?' Awasthi starts as they hit the highway.

'You must have a story to tell...' says Naveen.

'Yes sir. According to the Mahabharata, when the Pandavas were exiled, Arjun brought the tree from swarglok for his mother, Kunti, who offered it in prayer to Lord Shiva, in the temple she had established in Barabanki's Kintur village, which also gets its name from Kunti. Another legend is that the Parijat tree was brought here by Lord Krishna himself. Once, Narada, the mischievous sage, presented the precious flower of a Parijat tree to Krishna, who then gave it to his wife Rukmini. When Satyabhama, another consort of Krishna, came to know of this, she got jealous and demanded to be brought the whole tree. Lord Krishna then fought a fierce battle with Indra to bring the tree to earth for his beloved wife, Satyabhama. That is how the Parijat tree came to be in Barabanki. This Parijat tree is a kalpavriksha. There is no other tree like this in India. Every Tuesday, people gather to worship the tree.

'When I am transferred, who will tell me such interesting stories, Awasthi?'

∞

Three kilometres before reaching the place, they are passing through the sugarcane fields, when suddenly they hear a gunshot—someone has fired a gun at the car. Naveen loses control, and the vehicle zigzags on the road before slowing down and hitting a felled tree on the road.

'Sir, someone has shot at us. Bend down, bend down, bend down,' Awasthi shouts and pushes down Jayanti in the back seat.

A bullet hits the windshield and then the statue on the dashboard, blowing it to smithereens.

Naveen bends down to take cover from the firing. Getting out of the car would be really unsafe. He takes a quick look and makes a mental note of the position of their attackers—they are well beyond the 20-yard range of his revolver.

'I wish I had an AK with me right now,' shouts Awasthi and fires his pistol. As he leans out, there is another round of gunshots from the attackers. Awasthi recoils, drawing back quickly into the car.

Naveen takes the lead, and using the car door for protection, he leans out to fire at them.

Another round of shots, but this time, closer to the car. Some of the bullets hit the rear window glass with a cracking sound.

There's a sharp cry from Jayanti. Naveen sees her fall from the seat.

Naveen gives a shout and starts firing again, hitting one of the attackers in the thigh. The other attackers freeze, watching the injured one spewing blood and writhing in pain. Then they all fire together at the vehicle and jump on their bikes, speeding off. Naveen jumps out of the car now and fires at the direction of the retreating motorbikes.

'Sir,' Awasthi calls. 'One of them was the guy who followed us to the KGMC.' He then starts coughing.

'Madarchod!' Naveen shouts.

Awasthi's coughing gets worse. 'Awasthi!' Naveen turns to see blood pouring out from Awasthi's chest. His eyes are now closing as he slumps down.

'No, no, no...Awasthi...Awasthi! Stay with me,' Naveen tries to wake him up. 'I'll not let anything happen to you. Please keep breathing, Awasthi. Just listen to me, just keep breathing. I'll take you to the hospital. Just stay with me, and I'll stop the blood.'

The more Awasthi struggles, the more blood oozes out of his wound. Naveen pulls out his phone and immediately calls the police station, quickly describing his location and asking them to send an ambulance.

Naveen runs over to Jayanti. She is unconscious. Her eyes are closed. Naveen's uniform is caked in blood and mud by now.

He takes out a handkerchief and holds it against Jayanti's stomach, where the bullet has hit her. 'Jayanti, we are going to the hospital. Please keep breathing. Okay?'

She does not nod.

'ARE YOU WITH ME?' he shouts.

She nods.

Naveen runs back to Awasthi on the front seat to put a piece of cloth on his wound and ties it with his belt.

'Just 10 minutes.'

Awasthi is choking on blood. Naveen checks his wounded hand and shoulder, and it pulses blood.

The ambulance siren can now be heard. It screeches to a halt near them. The attendants come running out and take both Jayanti and Awasthi to their vehicle, where they are given emergency care. They then rush back to the Sanjivani Hospital in Barabanki on the Lucknow–Faizabad highway for the initial treatment.

Later, both of them are transferred to the Chandan Hospital, Lucknow, so that Awasthi's family can easily visit him.

∞

Naveen is waiting at the hospital with Raghav and Awasthi's family. After two hours, one of the two doctors comes and calls Naveen. He runs towards the doctor.

'We were able to save Jayanti,' the doctor says. 'Unfortunately, your colleague, Awasthi, got two bullets in the chest. We really tried our best, but we could not save him. I am sorry.'

Awasthi's wife runs inside the ward, sobbing, unable to control herself.

Naveen is dumbstruck. He follows her. The doctor and nurses have been able to stop the crimson blood from dripping down his wounds, but the scrapes and bruises tell how bravely he fought, without caring for his life. Naveen comes out of the room and sits on the bench near the door. He puts his head in his hands, and then punches the wall with a groan, scraping his knuckles so that they bleed.

Raghav steps forward and puts a hand on his shoulder to comfort him. He has never seen his strong cousin this emotional in his entire life. But he has lost a friend. There is something in that suppressed cry, a pain behind it.

'He never questioned me. Whenever I asked him to do something, he never asked whether there was a risk to his life. And I couldn't save him...I lost him, Raghav.'

Raghav pats his shoulder.

'He used to say that, sir, I am more connected to you than anyone else in the department. When I told him I could be transferred anytime, he told me he would be happy to go with me if it was possible. It's all over now.'

Naveen wipes his tears and asks, 'How's Jayanti?'

'Doctor said she is out of danger but will have to stay in the ICU for two days. We cannot meet her right now.'

The breaking news starts flashing on the TV screen in the lobby, reporting from the location of the incident.

A car ploughed through the jungle on the Lucknow–Faizabad highway today. Uttar Pradesh Police is trying to determine whether it was a terrorist attack. This has been a brutal attack on the police vehicle, nothing like in the past.

There was a girl in the vehicle along with SP Naveen Mishra. Sub-Inspector Awasthi suffered a life-threatening injury and was hospitalized. He has succumbed to his injuries. The police department has not confirmed anything yet about the attack. The incident has stirred public speculation over a possible threat to the safety of people in Uttar Pradesh.

Incidents like these just before the election make it

more challenging for political parties to convince the people that they are safe.

The DCP, who has just arrived, walks up to Naveen and asks, 'Who were these people? Any suspects?'

'I think we were being followed for many days. Awasthi identified one of them. We caught him a day before in front of KGMC disguised as a hawker. They are Ansari's people.'

∞

It's almost midnight. The DCP, DIG, Naveen and Verma are standing in a row in front of a funeral pyre. Their faces, dry and in deep sorrow. The police department has come together to mourn one of the most pleasant, likeable and hardworking policemen's tragic demise. He may not have been at a very high rank in the department, but he was always chosen for every operation in the last few years simply because of his personality. This is the funeral of a policeman who holds stories, accomplishments. But it is also a celebration of his life.

The DCP keeps his hand on Naveen's shoulder, 'Everyone goes through pain, and we can never escape this truth. We all lose people, and we all feel that pain. It's a tough time for everyone. We have lost a most brilliant man, and no one can ever replace him. Please help his family and let me know if I can do anything for them.'

Naveen just nods blankly without saying anything. He then just turns and leaves the funeral. The DCP asks Verma to make sure that he is fine.

Verma follows him to console him.

'Naveen...' Verma calls out to him.

Naveen pauses.

'Naveen, come with me, let's go home,' Verma says.

'I am fine. I need to attend to some unfinished tasks,' Naveen responds and waits for Verma to go back before he walks away.

'I understand your emotions, but don't do anything that risks your life.'

'Sir, without our rage, they treat us as the carpet on which they walk. We are police officers,' Naveen replies. Anger boils in Naveen like lava.

'Are you coming with me?' Naveen asks Verma.

'But where are you going?' Verma asks in confusion.

'They need to get the return gift, are you coming with me?' Naveen asks again.

'Yes, I am coming with you,' Verma says.

Naveen rushes inside the police vehicle with fury and hatred oozing out of his narrowed eyes and stony expression. They end up in Mawai.

seventeen

21 January 2022. 8.00 a.m.

BREAKING NEWS!

Four men, 27-year-old Kallu, 29-year-old Babloo, 22-year-old Aatif and 39-year-old Aalam, were shot dead last night at a shootout at Mawai.
    Mawai Police Station has not released any confirmation regarding the shootout.
    A day before, Sub-Inspector R.K. Awasthi was killed in an attack by a few local gangsters. However, the DCP and DIG have avoided speaking on the incident and are investigating the whole matter.

As Jayanti stirs, Naveen changes the channel before she can catch any of the news. His eyes fall on the monitor, showing the little beeps with her heartbeat. A drip has been set up to administer intravenous medicines.

The room smells strongly of a sterile chemical sanitizer. Jayanti smiles. Her face is swollen from being in bed for so long, but she tries to look normal.

She sits up and leans on the headboard.

'How are you feeling now? Where is Raghav?' asks Naveen.

'I am feeling much better now. Raghav did not know that you were coming. He just left for an errand. He must be coming soon,' Jayanti says.

'Naveen, Awasthi sir…'

Before Jayanti says anything further, Naveen tries to change the discussion, 'Doctors have said that you can go home tomorrow or day after. So, rest well and get well soon. Are you going back to the hostel?'

'No, Raghav asked me to stay with him at the hotel where he is staying until I feel better.'

'Sounds good.'

'Anyway, Raghav has already told me about Awasthi sir. He is no more. I know.'

Naveen comes close to her and puts his hand on the side support of the bed, 'The doctors tried their best. You don't worry about that. Get well soon. I am getting a call from the office. I'll meet you soon.'

Naveen leaves the room to avoid breaking down in front of Jayanti. He takes a pill from his pocket, swallows it dry and leaves the hospital.

∞

DCP Harsh Vardhan is waiting for Naveen while watching the news on YouTube in his cabin.

'May I come in, sir?' Naveen asks before entering.

'Naveen, please come,' the DCP settles in his chair and pauses the news.

'Thank you, sir.'
'How are you? How's your friend...Jayanti? Sit.'
'Fine, sir.'
'Naveen, I know you are hurt. We all are. But you should have at least told me what you were going to do! You risked your life. Do you know that?'
'Sir, if you want, you can suspend me for this. Anyway, I don't think I will be able to work on this case any further.'
'I would have definitely suspended you for that, but I also want the perpetrators to be punished. But not as revenge, not emotionally...'
'Sir, they shot him in the chest. It was brutal.'
'I understand. But the city must be at peace. These shootouts and encounters will only stir fear among the people. Let's be on standby and let people come out of this shock. I'll update you. If you want, you can take a day off and rest.'
Naveen nods, 'Okay, sir.'
'Naveen...' says the DCP.
Naveen turns.
'You are a brave officer. Don't risk your life like this again.'
Naveen smiles and leaves his office.

∞

Raghav opens the window at the hospital to let some fresh air in. Jayanti's eyes dart towards the window, and she sees a bare tree branch silently swaying in the breeze. Replacing her thumb with a bookmark, Jayanti shuts the book that Raghav has given her, which she has been reading to feel better.
Raghav's cellphone buzzes.

'Hello, Raghav, where are you? We may need some help from Jayanti. Can you ask her? I tried calling, but her number is not reachable,' Naveen says in a rush while walking out of the police station.

'I'll just come in a minute,' Raghav tells Jayanti. She nods and Raghav comes out of the hospital room.

'I told Jayanti to switch off her cellphone. I am here with Jayanti at the hospital. She must stay away from this.'

'I am very close to cracking the case and just want to expose Ansari.'

'Okay, wait then.'

Raghav goes back inside the room and puts his phone on speaker.

'Guys, I need help from both of you. Jayanti, if you want, you can opt out. But Raghav, I need you.'

'Tell me,' responds Raghav.

'You know someone from News24, right?'

'Yes, Archana Mishra.'

'Yes, Archana. I want you to request her to broadcast the news about all the suspicious activities happening inside IEC if she can. If she needs any evidence, she can ask me, and I'll provide it to her. You don't need to tell this to anybody, and neither does she have to.'

'Okay,' says Raghav, nodding slowly. 'I'll talk to her.'

'Jayanti, you had told me about your cousin, Prashant. He is from the same place. Ask him if he can be of any help,' Naveen says.

'I'll ask him,' she replies.

'As soon as any news channel covers it. I'll take care of it going viral on social media.'

'Are we not risking the careers of thousands of students? UGC will blacklist the college.'

'There is always collateral damage, Jayanti. Don't worry. UGC will never harm the future of 3,000 students. You can trust me on that.'

'Hmm, okay…one day this will be busted for sure if not today, so let's do it,' affirms Jayanti.

'Thank you so much, guys.'

∞

'Archana, how can you do something this big just based on a tip from some stupid person?'

'Don't call my sources stupid, Mohan. My sources are not like you, and they are common people. Let me do my job.'

'You are the face of the channel. Don't do anything stupid that degrades your image and that of the channel. This is very, very risky.'

'Mohan, what if this works out? Think of that. Don't be a coward. That's what I don't like about you.'

Archana turns to the rest of the team. 'Team, get ready.'

'Ma'am, we are going live in three minutes.'

'Okay, done,' Archana replies.

Mohan, the news director, remains standing, watching her take a seat in front of the camera.

Very good evening, and welcome to News24. You are watching the breaking news where you watch the biggest stories of India and the world. My name is Archana Mishra, and today's breaking news is from the most prestigious educational institute in Uttar Pradesh. This is exclusive news you are watching only on News24.

Today, we got a tip from our sources that there is a racket of counterfeit medicines being run from a construction site within the Indian Engineering College premises in Lucknow. When we asked the college administration to comment on this accusation, they simply refused to give any clarification. When our team reached the college, the college administration stopped us from entering, which increased our suspicion.

Avoidance is always a nod to things we cannot accept ethically and legally. There is also an apprehension that a professor from the college is involved in this. Shabaj Ansari, who is a chemistry professor in IEC, seems to be the mastermind of this racket.

News24 appeals to the dean and vice chancellor to break their silence on this matter.

If educational institutes like the IEC become the hub of such illegal activity, what can we expect from other institutes? News24 also appeals to the UGC to look into this matter and confirm that our brothers and sisters are in safe surroundings.

As soon as the news is over, Mohan calls Archana outside the newsroom.

'What are you doing, Archana? Do you even know the consequences?'

'Mohan, if this is wrong, you will have my resignation on your table tomorrow morning, okay?'

'Okay.'

Mohan remains silent, 'You always look overconfident. Beware of that attitude.'

'That's not overconfidence, Mohan. It's called trust. Trust your sources. The friendship. Unfortunately, you will never understand this because you have never tried that. You always run behind TRP and weekly rankings,' Archana pats on his shoulder, 'I'll see you around.'

eighteen

22 January 2022. 9.00 a.m.

Ayodhya, a place where people seek solace from the vicissitudes of worldly life. The greed and delusion people see in the world are driven by things such as joy and sorrow, honour and guilt, and profit and loss. This ashram, however, has all the qualities that most people want. A sign of a good ashram is its insistence on simplicity and solitude.

Ansari reaches Guruji's ashram and waits for his turn to meet him. A disciple of Guruji shows him the way to Guruji's room.

Guruji asks everyone to leave when Ansari enters.

'What happened, Ansari? What has brought you here? You are coming in the news these days, I hear?' Guruji looks at him and smiles.

'Guruji, only you can help me. I am stuck in a situation. These police officers are troubling me. If you talk to them once, it will be helpful for me. I'll be underground until the elections are over. I have been your follower and have always given you all my support, and I always will. Please help me out of this, Guruji. Please! They are investigating the case and getting involved in my personal life. My son and wife are being followed by the police.'

'That's why you should always avoid violence, Ansari! It's up to you what you choose, and you must decide whether to choose greed or faith. Greed will take you to hell, but by choosing faith, you will join me. But you have already chosen greed.'

'Guruji, it's a very small thing for you. Just call the ministry, and then this DCP will shut up.'

'You are thinking too fast, Ansari.'

'Guruji! I have talked to the dean. We are also talking to UGC to have one compulsory subject of yoga, with your branding on it, included in the curriculum. All are in full support of seeing you as our next CM.'

'Who all? Your community?' asks Guruji.

'Yes,' responds Ansari.

'Hmm,' Guruji nods and adds, 'I'll talk to the DCP. You go now. I'll also have to leave for a Bhoomi Poojan ceremony. Why don't you come and join the ceremony?'

'How can I join the ceremony?' says Ansari.

'Oh! How can you join! Anyway, it's a festival and there is huge media coverage over there, you better go and don't come until I say so.'

'Yes, Guruji. I'll leave for Lucknow. Please help!' says Ansari.

'Okay.'

∞

Guruji is sitting with all the holy men from the country, and this high-profile gathering is happening under a large open-sided temporary pavilion installed for the prime minister's speech.

There is high-end security everywhere.

This is a historic day. The whole country is delighted and emotional, and crores of people can't believe that they are experiencing this day in their lifetime. The great Ram temple will be a modern symbol of our culture, endless faith and national spirit and inspire humanity forever, as Lord Ram belongs to all of us.

Suddenly, loud voices start roaring...

> *Siyawar Ramachandra ki Jai!*
> *Siyawar Ramachandra ki Jai!*
> *Jai Siyaram! Jai Siyaram! Jai Siyaram!*

Sitting in an old armchair, legs crossed and fingers intertwined over one knee, Guruji calls the DCP from the other end of the pavilion, where he is supervising the security arrangements.

The DCP walks over, leans forward and greets him, saying, 'Guruji, *charan sparsh.*'

'Many congratulations for this auspicious day,' says Guruji in a loud voice.

'Thank you. We are all happy for this day,' responds the DCP.

'May God bless you! I wanted to talk to you about what is happening these days.'

The DCP nods.

'DCP, the ball is neither in my court nor in yours. The ball is going away from the court. When the ball goes out of the court, either you can take it back or leave it. In this case, we can't take it back because it will question my dignity and of the people who want to see me in politics. We want politics, not violence. Elections are on the way.'

'We are trying our best, Guruji.'

'DCP, you must maintain peace in this state, especially in Lucknow and surrounding towns because if any religious violence occurs in this city, it will spread across the country. It would be best if you stopped it right now. There are thousands of cases pending. Arrest some politicians of the opposition party and close it. What's his name? That inspector who came to my ashram in Ayodhya.'

'Naveen Mishra. He is a good cop, Guruji.'

'Then assign him to do your work. And DCP, keep the college away from all this. Bring the videos down from YouTube. The college is for education, and I am a trustee of the college.'

'Sure, Guruji. I'll see what I can do.'

'You can do your best. God bless you! *Jai Shri Ram!*'

∞

A press conference has been organized involving all the leading print and electronic media reporters. They have been invited to cover the critical news about the state's biggest challenge in the illegal business of counterfeit medicines. The DCP is addressing the press conference—sharing details of the biggest news in this case, the arrest of Ansari, a respected professor of IEC.

> *Ansari was going to Dewa Shareef Dargah, the pilgrim town of Dewa situated just 42 kilometres from Lucknow and 12 kilometres from the district headquarters of Barabanki, when he was held by security personnel. Barabanki Police were informed, and they were able to identify him. Ansari tried to escape from Dewa Shareef Dargah towards the*

village, but the Barabanki Police successfully arrested him. The police have apprehended him and his interrogation is underway.

The STF team has confirmed that Ansari has 470 acres of land in Barabanki worth rupees 156 crore. This land was acquired illegally by threatening and sometimes murdering the original owners. The land was used for his primary business of illegal drugs. Illegal weapons and oil were also stored and traded there.

At least 156 weapons have been seized and deposited. At least 17 gangsters running illegal businesses in association with Ansari have been identified, and action is being taken against them.

Apart from the Barabanki Police, the UP Police and STF team have taken action against Ansari's mafia kingdom in Jaunpur, Faizabad and Haidergarh.

Last night, under the lead of SP Naveen Mishra, the Uttar Pradesh Special Task Force team first raided Ansari's Barabanki location. The team seized 1,838 bottles of fake syrup, weighing 450 millilitres each, from a godown of another pharma firm based in Etawah and Kanpur, Uttar Pradesh. As much as 35,000 kilograms of chalk have been confiscated. This was being used to produce counterfeit medicines.

We all know India is the primary source of counterfeit pharmaceuticals traded worldwide, and the gang was very active during the pandemic and supplied counterfeit medicines in India and beyond our borders. They are also involved in drugs for malaria, HIV/AIDS, cancer, counterfeit antibiotics, painkillers and fake lifestyle drugs.

Barabanki was the central hub where the gang operated and was in contact with other gangsters.

A few men from Ansari's gang attacked the STF team during the raid, in which a few officials were injured. They are being taken care of in the government hospital and are currently out of danger.

The STF team has also done a great job and received a massive stock of 55,000 barrels of stolen oil, which they were using for transportation. They have also seized three empty tankers, 56 drums, 37 drums of diesel, 560 empty drums, and a suction machine and a packing machine. The gang was stealing oil from private tankers transporting the product from the outlets of public-sector oil companies in other states. The gang used to take out 100–200 litres of petrol from each tanker passing by and replace it with spirit. They did the same thing with diesel tankers, replacing diesel with water. The stolen fuel was further adulterated with spirit and smuggled to petrol pumps in smaller areas. We are also connecting with police from other states to take necessary action and find the links between these activities.

Both the locations belong to a local farmer of a village, and the land was given to Ansari on lease. Ansari was using the land as the hub of all his illegal activities. Looking at the movement of the gang, Uttar Pradesh Police will continue the search and raid any other locations until we clean the state.

The administration has also sealed the properties worth rupees 58 lakh of one Brijesh Pathak, Ansari's bodyguard and shooter.

> *The officials are now interrogating the arrested gangsters and investigating who else is involved in the illegal business of counterfeit medicines.*
>
> *Thank you.*

∞

It's 11.30 at night by the time Naveen reaches the DCP's home. He sits on the sofa in the waiting room decorated in pastel hues that soothe the soul. He looks around the pastel chairs and scattered cushions, just enough order and chaos—true perfection. The guard informs the DCP about his arrival.

'Hello, Naveen, come. I'll take you on a walk. Be comfortable. It's not formal at all,' says the DCP.

'Sir, was there anything urgent. Is everything all right?' asks Naveen.

'Naveen, we need to stop everything right now.'

'Yes, sir, that's what I want. We are almost there. I just need a day or two, and then we can submit the case to the court. This is the strongest case. Sir, Section 302—murder, and Section 307—attempt to murder, are enough to put Ansari and his men behind bars. There will be at least life imprisonment or death sentence. There are more charges, sir,' Naveen says.

'This is all okay. You have done great work, Naveen. Tell me, have you done an encounter before?' asks the DCP.

'What do you mean, sir?' asks Naveen, shocked.

'Have you done an encounter before?'

'Yes, once, with my team in Ayodhya. We took down five terrorists.'

The DCP pauses. Then he says, 'I am giving you a free hand to encounter Ansari.'

'What, sir?' Naveen is shocked. 'But, sir, Ansari has already been arrested, and I have all the evidence against him. We have a really good case.'

'Evidence can be fabricated or erased anytime. You are not new to that. Ansari is a threat to all of us, and he will find his way out of this, even when it's not looking good for him. You have to do this encounter. Submit the report to me in the next 24 hours.'

'Sir!'

'Do it while taking Ansari for interrogation from Barabanki to Lucknow. And remember, I don't want any loopholes. I need a clean report on my table tomorrow.'

'Sir, but the dean of IEC will also be with him...'

'The dean will be collateral damage. You will lead the team, and this should be your best shot. Get your team ready, and get all the information from Verma and others if needed. We have the confirmation. Go now, you don't have much time. It is a distance of an hour or so from Barabanki to Lucknow. You will have an hour. Plan accordingly.'

'Yes, sir,' Naveen salutes the DCP and turns to leave.

'Naveen,' the DCP approaches him. Naveen turns.

'Yes, sir?'

The DCP keeps his right hand on his shoulder and says, 'You are the best officer I have seen. I am proud of you, Naveen. All the best! Take a day off after that and have fun. I'll take care of you properly.'

'Sure. Thank you, sir.'

Naveen rushes from there. He forms a team of seven people

and a backup team. As the sun rises, the special team leaves for the assigned mission. Maybe the story of a criminal in Uttar Pradesh ends today.

There will not be any medals given to those officers, there will not be promotions, and there will not be any names in the media to talk about. There will be just breaking news flashing on the television next day.

∞

It's afternoon the next day at Taj Mahal Hotel, Lucknow, overlooking the beautiful Gomti River. Naveen and Richa are lying side by side on the bed.

'I love you so much, Richa. I was thinking, we're ready for the next step. What do you think?' says Naveen, holding his girlfriend Richa in his arms. They are blessed to have been together from their college days. Naveen has just got back from work, and they are meeting after a long time, as Richa had been studying in the US.

There is a calmness, a serenity, a feeling of optimism.

'Really?' she responds gently, her head on his shoulder.

'Yes.'

'I'm ready to spend the rest of my life with you, so yeah, let's go ahead. That is the most romantic thing anyone has ever said to me. I love you too.'

He laughs and grabs her shoulder. She suddenly turns him over.

'This time, I'm in control, so you be a good boy and don't move your hands. I'm going to drive you crazy, stop, and do it all over again until you beg me to finish this. Even then, I won't. I'm just gonna do every naughty thing to you until your mind and body explode.'

'No, no, no,' Naveen can't stop laughing before being seduced.

The news flashes on the TV while Naveen and Richa are lying in bed.

> *Good afternoon and welcome! Today is the day not just the whole police department was waiting for but also the public of Uttar Pradesh. The story of Ansari is over. This is Ranjana Kapoor bringing you the most sensational news of the country.*
>
> *Today, early morning, gangster Ansari has been killed in an encounter by the Uttar Pradesh Special Task Force (STF). Ansari was being transported from Barabanki to Lucknow when the police vehicle carrying Ansari was overturned, and Ansari tried to escape. Ansari nabbed a police weapon and opened fire at the police but was surrounded.*
>
> *In the gunfire, Ansari shot at the dean of IEC, who was also in the vehicle, and he died on the spot.*
>
> *Ansari suffered a few bullet shots in the retaliatory fire. Later, he was taken to a hospital in Lucknow, where doctors declared him dead.*
>
> *A few days ago, Ansari's men attacked a police vehicle on the Lucknow–Faizabad highway, in which one officer lost his life, and one other was injured. Several cases were registered against him.*
>
> *DCP Harsh Vardhan has confirmed that two police constables and two officers have also sustained injuries and*

are recovering well in the hospital.

Yuva Party president Bacchu Yadav has questioned the Uttar Pradesh government after the alleged encounter by the police.

Yadav tweeted: 'The car hasn't overturned, but the government has been saved from being overturned because of secrets and people behind it.'

The CM earlier promised that he would eliminate crime from Uttar Pradesh. Two hundred and seventy-nine encounters have been done in the last two years. The Opposition has made accusations that Ansari had political connections with both the parties in Uttar Pradesh.

Our prime minister is promoting the Swachh Bharat Mission, while our CM has taken it very seriously to clean the state of crime.

Signing off for today! Thank you!

'See, Mr Police Officer, your department has done a wonderful job. Who was leading the team? Must deserve a medal.'

Naveen nods, 'Does not matter. These operations don't need medals. It's my day off today.'

nineteen

A few weeks later...

'Case number 137, State Vs Shabaj Ansari,' a voice echoes in the court.

'The ultimate object of the criminal proceedings is to punish the accused on his conviction. A criminal court cannot continue proceedings against a dead person and find him guilty. Therefore, the criminal proceedings abate on the death of the accused, as their continuance after that will be infructuous and meaningless. Case number 137 is closed now,' declares the judge.

Mr Vinod Pandey, who is presenting this case stands up, 'Your honour, this may be happening for the first time in history that three closed cases will be discussed to prove deceased Shabaj Ansari is guilty. However, your honour, the motive is to establish the genuineness.'

'We are making history by solving three cases in a day, isn't it? Other courts must learn from us.' The judge smiles and adds, 'Proceed with the next case.'

∞

Case number 3202 – State vs Prakash Shukla

Mr Pandey starts, 'Your honour, I would like to call upon a witness in the Prakash Shukla murder case, which was reopened with the permission of the honourable court.'

'Please proceed quickly.'

'I would like to call our chief witness, Ramakant Yadav, to the stand, my lord,' Mr Pandey motions towards Naveen to bring in the old man.

Jayanti turns, a cold chill running through her spine.

Ramakant comes to the stands.

Mr Pandey comes forward and asks him to repeat whatever he confided to the police.

'Sahab! I know both of them, Prakash and Ansari. Prakash was well-educated and well-spoken. Before joining the police, Prakash was Ansari's right hand in his rallies when Ansari won the elections to the Zila Panchayat. After he joined the police, Ansari became stronger because now he had a true friend and his power. There were cases where Ansari was guilty, but Prakash helped him out of many situations because Prakash was blindly trusting Ansari. When Prakash came to know the truth about Ansari and his illegal rackets, he tried to stop him, but then it was too late. Not just Prakash but many officers from the police department used to come and have tea and dinner with him. Prakash was in shock because he was equally guilty of crimes in which he saved Ansari. Ansari and Prakash had some arguments. Ansari even threatened his family. After that, Prakash decided to resign from the policeforce. That was the biggest mistake he made. Leaving the police department convinced Ansari that Prakash was a threat to Ansari, and so he got him killed. Many people knew, but no one had courage to speak against him…'

'That's all, your honour,' Mr Pandey says.

The judge gives his final verdict before closing the case, 'A criminal court cannot continue proceedings against a dead person and find him guilty. Therefore, the criminal proceedings abate on the death of the accused, as their continuance after that will be infructuous and meaningless. Case number 3202 is closed now.'

Case number 138 – State vs Asim Ansari S/O Shabaj Ansari

Asim knows he has to appear confident. Otherwise, standing in the courtroom, it does not matter whether you are right or not. You are roasted, and the only thing that matters is how you can withstand the cross-questioning.

Both the lawyers stand up and take permission to proceed.

'Prosecution proceed,' the judge says.

'Thank you, your honour,' Mr Pandey says and proceeds, 'I want to ask a few questions. Do I have your permission, my lord?'

'Permission granted.'

Mr Pandey calls Asim to the stand.

'So, Asim, where were you that day when Ajay was found dead in the hostel?' asks Mr Pandey.

'I do not know where I was because I do not know when he was found dead in the hostel, but yes, I reached the hostel as soon as I heard that he was dead,' he says.

Asim's lawyer, Mr Tiwari, gives the judge the post-mortem report, the copy of the college register and some other documents found in Ajay's room. The judge goes through the documents and turns to the page where the cause of death is written: head trauma, internal bleeding and complications of a bone fracture.

Mr Pandey continues, 'Your honour, I would also like to throw some light on the post-mortem report, where it says there was a substantial amount of calcium carbonate, a chalk-like content found in his body. The substance did not affect the body in the last 48 hours. This is the same substance found in Ansari's Barabanki location, the same substance found behind the college cafeteria. This is not a coincidence, my lord,'.

The judge nods and writes something on the notepad, and says, 'Mr Pandey, the Supreme Court has ruled that separate trials must be conducted for cross-cases lodged by two parties involved in an offence, even if the prosecution witnesses are the same for both sides, as law prohibits taking into consideration evidence in one case for the cross-case. The evidence of one case cannot be used in another case, the case 137 is closed.'

'Your honour,' Mr Pandey bends partially in acceptance. The judge nods.

'So, Mr Asim, some of the students from the college said that Ajay never liked you. Can you tell us the reason for not liking you?' asks Pandey.

'I disagree. Ajay and I were good friends.'

'Okay, but what made you take the transfer from this campus to another campus?' asks Mr Pandey.

'That is just a coincidence.'

'Maybe,' Mr Pandey responds and adds, 'Your honour I would like to throw some light on the other side as well that though the racket of counterfeit medicines was run by Shabaj Ansari, his son Asim clearly had a motive to be a part of the racket by engaging other students like Ajay into this. Calcium carbonate can be a very common substance to find, but this common substance found just in line with the suspects, can be a rare coincidence.'

Mr Tiwari pitches in and says, 'Your honour, Mr Pandey has forgotten that judgements are given on the basis of evidence and proof, not suspicion or probability.'

Mr Pandey continues, 'I understand, your honour, but is it also a coincidence what was found when we recovered cellphones from Barabanki in the case 137? When the police retrieved the call list for those number, there was a repeated number in the call list. Do you know whose number it was? Of course, not yours. You are the son of Ansari, and you can't be so stupid.'

'Please come to the point, Mr Vinod Pandey,' the Judge says.

'Yes, your honour. So, the police called that number back, but the number was switched off, but the exciting thing was, its last location was IEC. To be precise, his house, your honour,' Mr Pandey says and looks at Asim to speak.

'I only have one number that the police is aware of,' Asim says with conviction.

The defendant's lawyer, Mr Tiwari, gets up from his chair and says, 'Honourable Court, with your permission. I trust whatever Mr Pandey is saying is correct, but all the questions he has asked does not prove that Asim has any connection with the death of Ajay Nagar,'

The judge looks at Mr Pandey and then asks the defendant's lawyer, Mr Tiwari, 'Mr Tiwari, would you like to share anything else in defense of Asim Ansari?'

'No, your honour. The questions my friend Vinod Pandey has asked do not prove anything. So, I would like to say that my client has committed no crime in Ajay's murder case, or you may call it a suicide case.'

'Your honour, I would like to remind my friend Mr Tiwari that this case is not just about Ajay's murder case, it also narrates the charges against him under Section 354(C) by the Criminal Law (Amendment) Act, 2013, which says viewing and/or capturing the image of a girl or woman in private is a criminal offense.'

This shocks the whole courtroom on how Mr Pandey smartly switches the context and proves him guilty on another account if not under Section 302.

Asim finds the courtroom suffocating. A few people are sitting in the pew, watching the proceedings, and many lawyers are patiently waiting for their cases to be called out.

Asim sees Jayanti and Raghav sitting in the pew as well. Their eyes meet. He quickly turns his face. Raghav holds Jayanti's hand to comfort her.

'Your honour, this is the written statement from the victim,' Mr Pandey passes the statement that Naveen took from Jayanti about her picture being made viral.

'Mr Pandey, do you have any other questions?'

'No, my lord, but I would like to look into all the evidence that clearly shows a link between Ajay's death and the counterfeit medicine racket, which was illegally run by Asim's father. However, we demand the judgement under Section 354(C) and request the honourable court to give us some more time to provide shreds of evidence in Ajay's murder case.'

'The prosecution has told the court that while there were no eyewitnesses in the case, the police had relied on circumstantial evidence to bring Asim to the court. The cardinal principle of criminal jurisprudence is that a case can be said to be proved only when there is specific and direct evidence, and no person can be convicted on pure moral conviction. Considering the discrepancies in evidence, the accused is undoubtedly entitled to the benefit of the doubt while setting aside the trial court order. However, under the Indian Penal Code, Section 354(C) by the Criminal Law (Amendment) Act, 2013, which says viewing and/or capturing the image of a girl or woman going about her private acts, where she thinks that no one is watching her, is a crime. The court punishes Mr Asim Ansari with imprisonment of one year with a fine of rupees fifty thousand. The honourable court also warns Mr Raghav and Ms Jayanti, under Section 294 of the IPC that prohibits the display of affection or any obscene act in any public place "done to the annoyance of others", to not repeat the nuisance.'

The court is adjourned. The judge hits the gavel.

∞

Jayanti and Raghav are standing at gate no. 5 of the Lucknow High Court, waiting for a cab to arrive. Raghav is going to the airport directly.

'You look much better today,' says Raghav.

'It's a day to look better,' Jayanti gives a most subtle and satisfying smile.

'You deserve a happy life. You have to take care of your health as well.'

She nods.

'So, when are you coming to Mumbai?' asks Raghav.

'Let's see if I get my work location as Mumbai, if and only if, I get selected.'

'You will, Jayanti,' Raghav speaks confidently.

'Even if I don't get placed anywhere. I'll figure out something for sure.'

'Of course, you will get something better because you are such a strong girl.'

'Thank you, Raghav.'

Raghav nods.

'I wanted to give it to you when you were leaving the college but couldn't...' Jayanti takes out a note from her handbag and gives it to him.

'What's that?' asks Raghav, taking the note and starting to read it.

Hi Raghav,

I want to say this to you, I don't wish for a strong man who can lift my spirits while I am at my lowest. I would be happy to be with a man who cries with me at my lowest. Two people in love living separately can't make two happy homes. Even if we fight together in one, it will make it more joyful than ever. I want to love you more than you ever did.

Yours forever,
Jayanti

Raghav starts laughing after reading the letter. 'Come here,' he pulls Jayanti close and hugs her.

'I love you. Well, I am not the same Raghav who you've written the letter to.'

'I know. You are a writer now. You can edit it accordingly.'

They both laugh and look lovingly at each other.

Epilogue

It's 11.00 on a December morning. On NH27, two police officers, SP Naveen Mishra and DCP Harsh Vardhan are on patrolling duty.

'Sir, do you know that Barbarik, son of Ghatotkacha, had a unique power. By Lord Shiva's blessings, he had special arrows with which he could mark his enemies and then destroy only them, without any other casualties. This could have ended the war in a minute flat. Krishna, however, knew better than to let this happen. Because of an oath to his mother, Barbarik always fought for the weaker side. Krishna appeared to him as a Brahmana and reasoned that whichever side he took would, by default, be more robust. That way, he would have to keep changing parties until everyone got killed. Krishna then asked for his head in charity because the battlefield must be purified before battle by sacrificing the head of the bravest Kshatriya. Barbarik obliged and became the greatest Kshatriya alive. That is how Krishna saved the Pandavas from losing the battle,' says Naveen.

'You must have heard this story from Awasthi, no?' DCP Harsh Vardhan asks.

'Yes, sir,' Naveen responds. After a pause, he says, 'Awasthi also told me this story. Once, Lord Krishna asked Barbarik for a proof of his abilities. He asked him to shoot every leaf present in an area filled with many banyan trees. Barbarik accomplished this with a single bow. Apparently, Lord Krishna had a leaf hidden under his feet. When he removed his feet, he found that leaf, too, was shot. Barbarik had never sinned in his life, so Krishna gave him a boon. Barbarik asked to watch the whole battle with his eyes. So, his severed head was put on a mountain so that he could watch whole battle of Kurukshetra.'

'You miss Awasthi a lot...' DCP says softly.

'I wish I could bring him back,' replies Naveen.

DCP pats his shoulder, 'Don't take so much stress, Naveen.'

Naveen switches on the newly installed mini TV on the dashboard.

'As he always wanted,' says Naveen.

The news flashes a press conference of Guruji:

> *I want peace in the state. There are several great people who have served this state. I never wanted to come into politics but the time has come, before we lose the dignity of this state and our religion. I declare that I am going to contest for the next election, and I need your blessings.*

'Sir, don't you think we only create differences? And then the entire system runs on those differences alone. Are we not losing its dignity?'

'White has no value when there is no black, Naveen, just as good has no value when there is no bad. Politics has no value if there is no religion associated with it.'

'What about people like Awasthi's family, your family, my family and the rest of the 140 crore people? Aren't they suffering because of this? *Sarve Bhavantu Sukhinah Sarve Santu Niramaya* means "May everyone be happy". It means that everyone, every animal, every person, every community and every atom, energy or creature should be happy and free from suffering. They all have equal rights to live in this city, in this country. *Muskuraiye, Aap Lucknow Mein Hain* (Smile, you're in Lucknow) has just become an idiom in the books, are we not losing the charm of it?'

'Yes, that's the ideal. But unfortunately, not everyone thinks like you.'

The DCP gets a call and is informed that the Commission of Inquiry has told the court that the entire version of the killing is concocted. The Opposition wants murder charges against the seven police officers involved, including the DCP.

'What happened, sir?' asks Naveen observing him curiously.

The DCP explains to Naveen what he just heard on the phone.

'That's funny. Now?' asks Naveen.

'Nothing. Let's go to meet Guruji! He is equally a part of it and now a stronger contender for the upcoming election.'

Acknowledgements

Firstly, I would like to thank my daughter, Anvika. Though she is too young to contribute to this book, I would like to thank her because she has changed me as a person, and she has made us realize how much our parents love us. So, on that note, I would like to thank my parents as well for all the love and care they have showered upon me. Also, my heartfelt gratitude goes to my wife for dealing with my mood swings. I owe you all every moment of my life.

Now, thank you to the beautiful city of Lucknow and its people. This city means a lot to me, and this city has been the place of my ancestors. I think I have not given back enough to the city in return for what it has given me. However, I wish to contribute to this city through my writings.

Now, coming to my family of readers, I hope you are healthy and enduring well. This is the first book after the pandemic, and we have lost many people. So, my deep condolences to all of you.

You all must have grown up, and I, too, have a few grey hair showing. So, I thought writing this book would bring something different to you, and I look forward to your views. Thank you for making me who I am today, and it is your love and blessings that encourage me to write. You all mean a lot to me. Stay connected. Keep smiling. See you, somewhere, sometime.